WILMOT AND CHIPS

"Well, go on then," Terry said. "What could you be famous for?"

"For having a brother who's a big twit," Wilmot said.

"I bet my brother's a bigger twit than your brother though," Terry said.

"I bet he isn't."

"Well, go on then. Tell me one thing you could ever be famous for. Go on. One thing then. Just one thing!"

"There's loads of things," Wilmot said. Then an idea came to him. "I could break a record," he said. "That's what I could be, a record breaker."

WILMOT

and

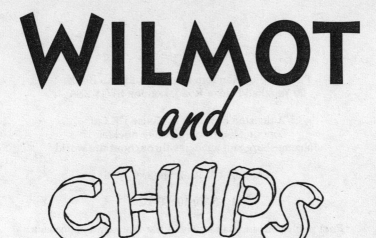

CHIPS

ALEX SHEARER

RED FOX

A Red Fox Book

Published by Random House Children's Books
20 Vauxhall Bridge Road, London SW1V 2SA

A division of Random House UK Ltd
London Melbourne Sydney Auckland
Johannesburg and agencies throughout the world

1 3 5 7 9 10 8 6 4 2

First published simultaneously in hardback and paperback
by Julia MacRae and Red Fox 1996

Phototypeset by Intype London Ltd

Printed and bound in Great Britain by
Cox & Wyman Ltd, Reading, Berkshire

Papers used by Random House UK Limited
are natural, recyclable products made from wood grown in
sustainable forests. The manufacturing processes conform to
the environmental regulations of the country of origin.

RANDOM HOUSE UK Limited Reg. No. 954009

ISBN 0 09 963821 5

To Nicholas and Kate

Contents

1

The Record Breaker

They turned off the television and sat thinking a while about the programme they had seen.

"I could be on television," Wilmot said.

"The only way you'd ever get on television would be if you sat on it," his brother Terry told him.

"I could be famous, don't you worry," Wilmot said. "I've got it in me."

"Got what in you?"

Wilmot wasn't really sure, but he thought he'd better say something.

"Talent," he said, "and unique abilities."

"Rubbish," his brother said. "You're just a scruffbag. And you're nearly bottom of the class."

"No, I'm not," Wilmot said. "I just sit at the back. Clever people always sit at the back."

"No they don't," Terry said. "It's all the muckers-

1

about who sit at the back. That's the only talent you've got, to sit there pulling faces."

"People who sit at the back of the class are always the intelligent ones," Wilmot said. "They already know what the teacher's talking about, so they sit at the back where they don't have to listen, in order to give all the stupid ones at the front a chance to get an education. That's why you sit at the front – 'cause you're ignorant."

"Then how come you got all your spelling wrong?" Terry said.

"It wasn't wrong," Wilmot said. "It was just different. It was back-of-the-class spelling. It was regional variations."

"Yeah," his brother said. "It was wrong."

"Anyway, I could be famous if I wanted to be. Quite easily."

"How?" said Terry. "What could you ever be famous for? The only thing you could be famous for would be for the fact that no one had ever heard of you."

"I could do great things if I wanted to," Wilmot said. "It's just a matter of putting your mind to it."

"Well, you'd need to get a brain first to do that."

"Well, there'd be no point in trying to borrow one from you. Your head's full of nothing. In fact, if you didn't pump it up every morning, you wouldn't have a head at all."

"I'm going to get you for that," Terry told him.

A third voice was heard then, coming from the direction of the kitchen.

"Boys!" it said. "Boys! Are you arguing?"

"No, Mum," Terry said, giving Wilmot a Chinese Burn.

"No, Mum," Wilmot agreed, and he kicked Terry in the shin until he let him go.

"Then don't!" their mother shouted. "If I hear you two fighting again, there'll be trouble!"

They fell silent until they heard the pans banging and clattering in the kitchen again.

"See," Wilmot said. "See what you've done!"

"See," said Terry, "see!" And he now gave his brother a Japanese Burn – something he had invented himself. It was very like a Chinese Burn. In fact, it seemed exactly the same. But Terry maintained that it was different, but he wouldn't say why because it was a secret.

"Ow!" Wilmot said. "Get off!"

"Japanese Burn, see," Terry said. "So watch it, or you'll get a Russian Burn next."

"Yes, well have an Irish Kick in the Shins, then," Wilmot said. And he kicked his brother in the shins again. An Irish Kick in the Shins did seem very much like any other kick in the shins. But

Wilmot said that there were differences and that an Irish Kick in the Shins was worse. But he refused to say why, as it was a secret.

The brothers sat for a few minutes while Terry gave Wilmot burns from round the globe and while Wilmot gave Terry international kicks in the shins. But then they tired of that and took a breather to recover from their injuries.

"I reckon I could be famous, though," said Wilmot, who was now quite taken by the idea, and who could already see his name up in lights, or even better, on the front page of the *Beano*.

"I thought that was Minnie the Minx," Terry said. But as he couldn't quite remember, he went hunting for an old copy among the newspapers.

"No, that's the *Dandy*. Anyway, I'd soon see her off," Wilmot said. "One good Norwegian Kick in the Shins and that would be the end of her."

"Well, come on then, what can you do?" Terry demanded. "You can't sing, you can't dance, you can't spell, you can't make your bed. So what can you do? You've got to be able to do something to be famous. You can't get famous for doing nothing. So what could you ever be famous for – apart from making horrible smells in the bathroom?"

"Belt up," said Wilmot. "Or I'll give you a German Poke in the Eye."

"Well, I'll give you a Welsh Burn, plus a Double Bumble Bee with Extra Stings, if you're not careful. So watch it."

Wilmot didn't know what a Double Bumble Bee with Extra Stings was, and he suspected that his brother didn't know either. But he didn't want to risk finding out, in case there really was such a thing. So he just said, "You don't scare me," and laughed nervously.

"Well, go on then," Terry said. "What could you be famous for?"

"For having a brother who's a big twit," Wilmot said.

"I bet my brother's a bigger twit than your brother, though," Terry said.

"I bet he isn't."

"Well, go on then. Tell me one thing you could ever be famous for. Go on. One thing then. Just one thing!"

"There're loads of things," Wilmot said. Then an idea came to him. "I could break a record," he said. "Yes, that's it. That's what I could be, a record breaker."

Terry's eyes narrowed, and he looked at his younger brother as though Wilmot might be getting one over on him. Terry hadn't thought of that, but yes, maybe it was just about possible. Wilmot was probably just about stubborn enough and

5

awkward enough and weird enough and stupid enough to go and set a record for something. And then they'd never hear the end of it. If that was what Wilmot was planning, he'd have to be stopped. He couldn't have Wilmot being famous – he'd be insufferable.

"Huh!" Terry said. He thought it sounded quite good so he said it again. "Huh!" he repeated. "You? Break a record? You? Huh!"

"I don't see why I couldn't break a record," Wilmot said snootily. "I broke that compact disc, didn't I?"

Yes, he had. And he was still paying for it out of his pocket money at twenty pence a week. It had been one of Dad's favourite compact discs, the one he used to play when he'd drunk two cans of lager, and Wilmot hadn't really meant to damage it, only he hadn't been able to find his frisbee, and a compact disc seemed like the next best thing. Obviously he hadn't expected it to go flying over the hedge into next door's garden and get entangled with Mr Ronson's lawn mower, but these things happen. Dad had said that the compact disc had cost him twelve pounds and that if Wilmot paid it off at twenty pence a week, then he should have paid it all off in about a year. So far Wilmot had only made two payments – but it was a start.

"No," he said, scratching his chin, which always meant that he was deep in thought, "I don't see why I shouldn't break a record at all."

2

Round the Garden

The problem was, which record to break.

After tea, Wilmot got the *World Book of Records* down from the bookshelf and had a look through it.

I wouldn't have minded being the first man on the moon, he thought. Pity it's already been done. I could have made history. I could have said something that people would always have remembered. Something like, "One little pair of feet for me, one great big pair of tootsies for all mankind." Or something.

Still, never mind. Maybe there was something else he could be first at – something athletic. He turned to the Sports and Games Records pages and looked at running – the one hundred metres. The book – which might have been a bit out of date, but that was a chance he would take – said that the world record for running one hundred metres was 9.86 seconds. Well, that didn't sound too difficult to beat. He'd have a go at that now. Now how far was one hundred metres? He ought to know, but he wasn't sure. Was it the very short race, or the very long one? He'd better go and ask Terry. He found him up in his room.

"Terry?" he said.

"What?"

"How far's one hundred metres?"

"Why do you want to know?"

"Because I'm going to beat the record."

"Oh, I see, yes right. Well, in that case . . . " and Terry looked wickedly out of the window, "I'd say that one hundred metres was probably about fifty times round the garden."

"Fifty times round the garden?" Wilmot said. One hundred metres was obviously a lot further than he thought.

"Maybe even sixty," Terry said. "Yes, more like sixty, probably. Umm, yes, sixty times round the garden, I'd say."

"Right," said Wilmot. "Thanks."

He went down to the kitchen and put on his shoes by the back door. His mother watched him.

"Where are you going?" she asked.

"Just out into the back garden," he said.

"Well, don't be too long. You've got to have your

bath." She looked at him suspiciously. "What are you going to do? You're not going to play Frisbee, are you?"

"No!" Wilmot said, in tones of injured innocence.

"Show me your hands."

He showed his empty hands so that she could see that there were no compact discs.

"Clean, see," he said. "Apart from the dirt."

"All right," his mum said. "Off you go."

"Can you time me?" Wilmot said.

"Time you? For what?"

"For running," he told her. "I'm going for the record."

"Oh," said his mother, in her 'here we go again' voice. "Oh, all right."

"Are you ready then?"

"Hold on," his mother said, "I'll set the oven timer. Okay. When you're ready."

"Count me down," Wilmot said.

"Three, two, one, off!" his mother said, anxious to get on with her cooking.

"Wasn't ready," Wilmot said. "Again."

"On your marks, get set, go!" his mum said. And this time he was really off. She shut the door on him, picked up her rolling pin and continued making pastry.

A few moments later, Terry sauntered in to the kitchen to get himself a drink of water. He looked out of the window to see Wilmot running round the garden as fast as he could go. Wilmot was counting the number of times round the garden he had run. And every time he passed the kitchen door, he increased his number by one.

"Six!" he shouted, as he went by the window. He was starting to look rather hot, but he kept going.

"What's Wilmot doing, Mum?" Terry asked, as if butter wouldn't melt in his pockets.

"Running," Mum said.

"Why?" Terry asked.

"Oh, I don't know. Some reason or other. Another of his daft ideas probably. He wants me to time him, that's all I know."

"He looks a bit red in the face," Terry said. "I hope he's not going to have a heart attack."

"I wouldn't think so," Mum said. "Not at his age. Now, I must get on with this baking."

Wilmot passed the window again.

"Eight!" he shouted. "That is, seven, I mean!"

"No cheating!" Terry shouted. "How long's he been running for, Mum?" he said, all innocence again.

"Four minutes," Mum said.

"Right," said Terry. And he wandered back off up to his bedroom to read his books.

Dad came home while Terry was upstairs

reading. He went to the kitchen first, to say hello to Mum and to make a cup of tea. While the kettle boiled, Dad opened the letters the postman had brought for him in the morning. He normally left the house before the postman arrived, and so didn't see his letters until he got back. He had just begun to open an envelope, when Wilmot ran past the window.

"Twelve!" Wilmot said.

Dad stared out.

"What's he doing?" he said.

"Running," Mum said.

"I can see that," Dad said, "but what's he running for? There's no one chasing him, is there?"

"Not as far as I know," Mum said.

"And where's he running to?"

"No where," Mum said. "He's just going round the garden."

"Thirteen!" Wilmot said, flashing by again.

"I'm supposed to be timing him," Mum said.

"So how long's he going to keep going?"

"I don't really know," Mum said. "Until he gets fed up with it, I suppose. Anyway, at least he's not under my feet."

"No, true enough," Dad said. And he sat down to read the paper.

"Fourteen!" Wilmot said, and he flashed by the window again. He didn't flash by as quickly this time though, but he was determined to keep going. He'd break that record if it killed him. He'd show Terry, he'd show them all.

Mum saw that he was starting to tire, and so she opened the window and called out.

"Wilmot," she said, "now don't overdo it, will you?"

"I . . . I . . . I'm . . . all right," he gasped.

"Well, bath time when you've finished," Mum reminded him.

"Fifteen," said Wilmot, and he shot by again. This one hundred metres was taking longer than he thought. What did he have to beat again? Nine and a bit seconds. He hadn't realised that a second was such a long time. He had thought that it was much shorter than this. But maybe he was getting seconds mixed up with minutes . . . or hours . . . or days . . . or even weeks. Maybe Terry was right, and he had spent too much time mucking about at the back of the class.

"Sixteen!" Wilmot counted, and on he went. Thank heavens he was only trying to break the record for the one hundred metres. Just think if he'd gone for the mile! Or maybe he had made a mistake. Maybe he had misread the record book, and it hadn't said nine and a bit seconds for the hundred metres, what it had really said was nine and a half hours for the marathon. But he kept going.

Wilmot looked up at the sky as he ran round the garden. It seemed to be getting darker. He hoped he'd finish before the sun went down. If he had to run in the dark, he might trip over a rabbit or something and break his leg. Not that there were any rabbits in their garden. Just a plastic garden gnome with a fishing rod.

"Eighteen!" Wilmot shouted, and on he went.

It was hard work, this record breaking.

3

Shorts on Fire

They were all in the kitchen watching him – Mum, Dad, and Terry, who had come back downstairs. Some of the neighbours were watching too, looking out from their kitchen windows, or their back bedrooms, and wondering what he was up to. Mr Ronson next door had actually come out to peer over the garden fence at Wilmot, and to give him advice.

"Keep those knees up, Wilmot!" he said. "Pace yourself."

"Fifty four!" Wilmot said, whizzing round again. "I think," he added, as he was afraid he might have lost count. He wished Mr Ronson wouldn't talk to him, it was distracting.

"I like to see a boy with an interest in athletics," Mr Ronson said, filling his pipe and getting settled in for a long talk. "Reminds me of when I was the

15

star runner for the Harpmeet Harriers. Did I ever tell you about it?"

"Fifty three!" Wilmot gasped, going round again. Had he said fifty three? Was that right?

"I ran a race that should have gone down in the record books," Mr Ronson was saying. "They say in the record books that it was Roger Bannister who was the first man to run a mile in under four minutes. Well, you can't believe what you read in record books. Because it wasn't him, not by a long pair of shorts, it was me."

"Forty nine," Wilmot counted, coming round again.

"What happened was that I was having a quick smoke of my pipe, just before the race started. Then they called for it to get underway and there I found myself, at the starting line, with this pipe in my hand and no where to put it and no one to give it to. So what did I do, you ask yourself?"

"Fifty eight!" Wilmot said, coming round once more, his lungs aching, his legs sore, his mind in a tangle.

"Exactly! There were fifty eight different things I could have done," Mr Ronson went on. "But I didn't do any of them. No, what I did was to put my pipe in the back pocket of my shorts. Because they had them in them days – shorts with back pockets. Front pockets too, some of them. And braces to keep them up. And they had much longer shorts then as well. In fact, some of them were so long, they were longer than your trousers. Oh yes, there was many a promising runner back then who came to grief because his shorts were too long and he fell over them."

"Fifty nine!" Wilmot said, and round again he went.

"Yes, that would be right," Mr Ronson agreed. "Nineteen fifty nine – or maybe it was forty nine – but anyway, so I put my pipe in the back pocket of my shorts, thinking it has gone out, and not realising that it is still smouldering. So off I run, and I get a few yards, when I feel this warm sort of sensation behind me. So I turn round, and I look, and there I am, with my bum on fire!"

"Fifty eight," Wilmot said. There was something going wrong somewhere. He was definitely losing count.

"That's right. Fifty eight of us in the race, and it would have to happen to me. Well, Wilmot," Mr Ronson said, "I don't know if your bum's ever caught fire, but you can take it from me, lad, that it's the sort of thing you don't forget in a hurry. And it's not as if you can even ring the fire brigade. Because by the time they'd arrive to put it out, you wouldn't have a bum left. So what did I do, you're wondering."

"Twenty two!" Wilmot shouted. He was definitely losing count, he was, definitely.

"Well, I'll tell you. I ran, that's what! I ran like the devil himself was after me. I ran straight over that finishing line, leaving all the others trailing, and I ran to the stall where the refreshments were all laid out, and there was this great big dish there, with a huge blancmange, and so I went and sat in it – just like that. And do you know, that was the best blancmange I've ever had in my life. I can't tell you how wonderful it felt, just to sit there with your scorched bum in cool blancmange. It's magic, a thing like that, Wilmot. I just hope that you can have a few experiences like that to look back on when you get to my age."

"Sixty!" Wilmot said.

"No, I'm sixty-five, as a matter of fact, lad, but you were close. Anyway, so that was how I became the first man to run the mile in under four minutes. In fact, I think I actually ran it in about five seconds. Well, nice to talk to you, Wilmot, I'll have to go in now, as my programme's on the telly, and I wouldn't want to miss it. Cheerio."

And Mr Ronson went into his house.

Wilmot was still running. He didn't know why. It had just become a habit now, and he couldn't seem to stop. But hang on! What had he just said?

Yes, *sixty*. He had done it. He stopped circling the garden and headed for the kitchen.

"Mum, Mum!" he shouted. "Did you time me? How long did I take?"

"Hang on," she said, and looked at the oven timer. "Twenty seven minutes. And take your shoes off before you come in, I don't want mud on the floor."

Wilmot couldn't believe it. "How long did you say?"

"Twenty seven minutes. Have you got cloth ears?"

"He's got a cloth brain," Terry ventured to say. But Mum and Dad both scowled at him, so he didn't say anything else.

"Oh, then I haven't beaten it," Wilmot said, as he sat on the kitchen steps to undo his shoelaces, his heart heavy with disappointment.

"Beaten what, Wilmot?" Dad asked.

"Broken the record," he said. "For the hundred metres."

Dad put down his paper and looked at Wilmot in astonishment.

"The what?"

"The hundred metres, of course," said Wilmot. "What did you think?"

"The hundred metres?"

"Yes," said Wilmot. "It was in the record book,

and I was trying to beat it." Terry began to stealthily move out of the kitchen. He was starting to think that maybe it was time he beat it as well. "The world record was nine and a bit seconds. Well, it's taken me twenty seven minutes. I don't think I've done very well, really."

"Just a minute, Wilmot," Mum said. "Who told you that sixty times round the garden was equal to a hundred metres?"

"He did," Wilmot said, and he pointed at his brother, who had made it as far as the doorway and was about to tiptoe out.

"Terry!" Dad said. "Where are you going?"

"Me?" Terry said. "Oh, just thought I'd stretch my legs."

"I'll stretch your neck if you don't come back here," Mum said.

"Something up?" Terry said, all innocence. He suddenly looked at his brother, as if he had only just seen him. "What's up, Wilmot?" he said. "You look hot. Have you been running?"

"Terry," said Dad. "What's the big idea? Telling your brother that one hundred yards is the same as sixty times round the garden?"

"Did I say that?" said Terry. "Surely not."

Wilmot was looking at his brother, open mouthed. It took a moment for the enormity of the deception that had been perpetrated upon him to sink in. But yes, it had happened once more. Terry had conned him again.

"Come here, Wilmot," Dad said. He took him to the kitchen door. "You see Mr Ronson's garden fence there?"

"Yes, Dad," Wilmot said.

"Well, from the door here to Mr Ronson's fence is about fifty metres. From the door here to Mr Ronson's fence and back is double that, about one hundred metres. But sixty times round the garden is more like ... well, I don't know ... miles."

"I thought it was taking a while," Wilmot said. "I thought there was something funny about it." He looked towards Terry. "It's him," he snarled. "He fitted me up!"

Terry realised that all eyes were upon him – Mum's, Dad's and Wilmot's. Mum's eyes were full of reproach, Dad's eyes were full of amusement, and Wilmot's eyes were full of hatred and revenge.

"Well, Terry?" Mum said. "Well?"

"I can explain," Terry said. "It was a mistake. I thought he asked how many times round the garden was equal to the *ten thousand* metres, not the hundred metres." He shrugged. "Simple misunderstanding, that's all." He turned to Wilmot. "Sorry, Wilmot," he said. "Really sorry little bros."

Wilmot didn't believe a word of it, and he suspected that neither did Mum nor Dad. But there was nothing he could do to prove it. That was the trouble with Terry, he was such a slippery character. Trying to pin Terry down was like trying to get hold of a jelly.

"Genuine mistake," Terry was saying. "Really, really sorry. Really, really, really, sorry."

"Yes, all right, Terry, thank you," Mum said. "No need to overdo it."

"Really sorry," he said. "Still, never mind, eh, Wilmot? You can't expect to win everything. Especially not on your first time out."

"Yes, well don't you worry. There'll be plenty more chances. I'll break another record. No problem," Wilmot said. "Right, I think I'll go and have my bath."

"Very sensible," Mum said. "You're a very sensible boy, Wilmot, that's a very good attitude to take."

"And at least I tried," Wilmot said.

"That's right," Dad agreed. "You did. Now shake hands you two, to show there's no hard feelings."

Terry looked a bit nervous. But Wilmot didn't need a second asking. He approached him openly and offered his hand in a friendly way.

"No hard feelings, Ter," he said. "Just a misunderstanding."

Terry gingerly took the proffered hand. "No hard feelings, Wilmot," he said, "just a mistake."

They shook hands while Mum and Dad looked on approvingly. But they didn't see Wilmot dig his thumb into Terry's hand, and nip the skin on the back of it. And they didn't notice Terry trying to squeeze Wilmot's fingers. And they didn't hear Wilmot as he leaned forward and said under his breath, "You're a marked man now, Terry. I'll get you for this."

4

Revenge Number One

Although Wilmot was the younger, there was only a year's difference in their ages, and in terms of size they were almost equally matched. Terry had the edge slightly, and was a little bit heavier and taller, but he knew that there was no room for him to relax his guard. Wilmot posed a serious threat, especially when he had the element of surprise. If Wilmot were to ambush him, Terry might not get the better of it. He decided, therefore, that it might be best if he slept with his tennis racket under his pillow. But Mum found it when she came up to say good night to him and she took it away.

When she went into Wilmot's bedroom, Mum also found that Wilmot was in bed with his cricket bat.

"I don't know what you two are up to," Mum

said. "But whatever you're thinking of doing, Wilmot, don't do it."

"I wasn't thinking of doing anything, Mum."

"No, not much." And she said good night.

Wilmot waited for ten minutes after Mum had gone downstairs, then he climbed out of bed and opened his door.

Terry heard the door squeak. He lay awake and listened, his eyes wide open. Then he saw the light come in from the landing as his own bedroom door began to open. He closed his eyes and feigned sleep, but he was alert and ready. He heard Wilmot's soft footsteps as they padded over the carpet. He waited until he heard him stop beside his bed, until he could feel Wilmot's breath as he leant over him, and then . . .

They both struck together!

"Hundred metres, eh?" Wilmot hissed. "Sixty times round the garden, eh? Well, you know what you get for that, don't you? You get an Egyptian Punch in the Pyramids."

"Oh, do I now," said Terry, blocking the Egyptian Punch in the Pyramids with a Welsh Stoppit, which he had invented himself. "Well, here's an African Ant Bite, and a Mexican Toe Strangle for you to think about." And he got Wilmot by the foot and gave his big toe a very painful twist.

"You've asked for it now," Wilmot said, his face

contorted with pain. "I shall have to unleash my deadly blows now. I'm afraid this calls for a Burmese Rabbit Thumper and a Jamaican Green Banana Thumpit with Double Spiders!"

So saying, he fell on Terry and did his best to give him a seeing to, while Terry did his best to defend himself, and to retaliate in kind. So involved were they in fending off blows and exotic strangleholds, that they didn't even notice that they had fallen off the bed, with a thump loud enough to bring the plaster down in the room below.

In fact they didn't even notice the door open, and they didn't even see Dad standing there, framed in the doorway, his brown hair looking strangely grey with little flecks of white plaster in it. And Terry was in the middle of giving Wilmot a Brazilian Bony Elbow, and Wilmot was giving Terry a Very Rare Clog in the Kidneys, all the way from the Netherlands, when Dad cleared his throat and said, "If you two don't stop fighting, and if you, Wilmot, don't get back to your own room, I will give you two such an Intergalactic Telling Off, you'll be seeing stars with your ears!"

And at that, they decided to call it quits, and to leave further arguing until another day.

Wilmot was not discouraged. If anything, his failure to break the world record for the one hundred metres had only whetted his appetite. Not that Terry was going to let him forget *that* in a hurry.

"A hundred metres in twenty seven minutes!" Terry said, as they walked to school the next morning. "I know snails who can run faster than that. I know grass that can grow faster than that. I know . . ."

"I don't want to know what you know, thanks very much," Wilmot said. "Because what you know doesn't seem to be very accurate, does it? But I'm still going to be famous, see, so don't you worry. And when I'm famous, and you're still just a big nobody who's no good at anything – like you are now – well, don't think I'll be having you on my chat show."

"What chat show?" Terry demanded.

"The chat show I'll have when I'm a celebrity," Wilmot told him.

"They wouldn't give you a chat show," Terry said. "You'd run out of things to say after five seconds. Dead boring, you'd be. Everyone would switch off."

"No, I wouldn't," Wilmot said. "I'd have interesting people on there."

"Such as who?"

"Well, not you for a start. You'd bore the pants off a nudist, you would."

27

"I'm not as boring as you," Terry said.

"It's you who's boring," Wilmot said. "I'm not boring at all. I'm dead interesting, I am. But you're so boring, you'd even put a plank of wood to sleep."

"It's you who's the boring one," Terry said. "In fact you probably hold the record for being the world's most boring person already."

"You probably hold the record for being the world's smelliest person," Wilmot said.

"You probably hold the record . . ."

But they were in the school playground by then and so split up to go their separate ways and to join their different friends in their class rooms.

Wilmot began to wonder if he really was the world's most boring person. It wasn't that he wanted to be, but it would have been a record. And he supposed that it was a sort of distinction in itself to be the most boring person in the world. If he really was the most boring person in the world, then he ought to get the credit for it, and his name in all the record books. He decided that he ought to get another opinion on the matter, and he stopped Steve Coombs in the corridor.

"Steve," he said. "Am I the most boring person in the world?"

"No," Steve said. "Mr Angelus the music teacher

is the most boring person in the world. But you come in a pretty close second. Why?"

"Oh, no reason. Thanks." And they went on their ways.

A close second in the boring stakes. It wasn't bad, but it wasn't quite good enough. Wilmot didn't just want to be a runner up, he wanted to be the top man in his own field. Second biggest bore just wasn't big enough. He would have to think of something else.

At break time, Wilmot discussed his plans with his friend Martin Fields, who thought that trying to get your name into the record books was a very good idea.

"Only what for?" Wilmot said. "That's the problem."

"How about telephone boxes?" Martin said.

"What?"

"Telephone boxes. I saw it in the *Believe It Or Not* on holiday. There's a world record for the number of people in a telephone box. You could try and break that."

"What, on my own?" Wilmot said, for it was individual rather than group distinction that he was yearning for.

"No, of course not on your own," Martin said. "One person on his own in a telephone box, what sort of record's that?"

"Well, how many do you need then? What's the world record at the moment?"

Martin squinted, screwed up his face and tried to remember.

"I think that it was something like . . . two thousand."

Wilmot's jaw dropped. "Two thousand?" he said. "Two thousand people? In one telephone box!"

"I think so," Martin said uncertainly. "Or maybe it was half a million. Or was it a billion?"

"A billion? A billion people? In one telephone box?"

Martin looked thoughtful. "Or was that the population of China? It was definitely one or the other. Definitely a record of some kind." His brow furrowed again, and he sucked his teeth. "Or maybe it was twenty seven."

"Twenty seven?" Wilmot said. "What, was it a Chinese telephone box then? Are they bigger?"

"No, no," Martin said. "They don't have to be Chinese. They can be anything. But that's the record. Twenty seven people in a telephone box . . . or was it balanced on a bicycle? Anyway, it was definitely a lot. I mean, more than you'd expect. So you could try that then – eh?"

"Thanks . . ." Wilmot said dismally.

"You're welcome," Martin said, going off to play handball.

". . . for nothing," Wilmot added when Martin had gone away.

Nobody was helping him at all, really. He could see that he would have to see this one through on his own.

Wilmot's conversation with Martin Fields set him thinking for the rest of the morning. He supposed that there were lots of records like that – for the most people in a telephone box, or the biggest crowd at a football match, or the most people to all hold hands and make a human chain. But things like that didn't appeal to him at all. He didn't want to be remembered as just one of many crammed into a telephone box. He wanted to be famous for something that he alone had done – something valuable and wonderful. Something he could be proud of for the rest of his life.

But what?

He tried to think of something all through the next lesson, but without success.

The bell rang for dinner break then, and Wilmot went to fetch his lunch box from the cloakroom where he had left it. He didn't much care for school dinners and so Mum always gave him and Terry a packed lunch. Today he could smell chips though, wafting through the assembly hall from the canteen.

And that was when it came to him.

31

He wondered what the world record was for eating chips. As far as he knew, there wasn't one. The record was there for the taking.

The World Record for Chips.

5

Chips

Wilmot was right. There was no record he could think of ever having seen in the record book at home for eating chips. None at all. Not one.

So that, maybe, was the answer. That was the road to fame and glory. You didn't have to try and beat an existing record, you simply set a new one of your own. And if in future years someone younger and fitter and with a bigger mouth came along and beat your record, what did it matter? In fact, that was only to be expected. The point was that you would have been the first, a pioneer. You would be the one to beat. Others would have to measure themselves against you. Your name would always be there.

Wilmot thought it all over as he walked back home, while his brother Terry followed behind him, trying to trip him up with a Saudi Arabian Sneaky Boots he had just invented. It wasn't proving very effective though, as Wilmot found it easy to foil with a Bavarian Kick in the Ankle which he had been deploying for some days now with great success. And by the time they got home, Wilmot was decided. He was going to go for the record, and he was going to make it unbeatable. He would show them all – and especially Terry. He was going to set the World Record for Chips, the record for the most chips ever eaten in five minutes. And everlasting fame would be his.

It was going to need some organising though, he realised that, and he would probably have to go into training. He would need a clock with a second hand, a time-keeper, a quiet place where he would not be interrupted – particularly not by adults, for Wilmot had a sneaky feeling that adults would not approve of his plans – and he would need an unlimited supply of chips. And for that, he might need money. Or maybe not. But he would certainly need potatoes.

Nevertheless, it was a sound scheme, and there was no reason why it shouldn't work. At the same time though, there was no sense, either, in letting past efforts go to waste. His sixty times round the garden had cost him a lot of sweat and toil, and he felt that it should be recognised.

So the plan was that the World Record for Chips attempt should be got underway as soon as possible. And in the meantime, his World Record For Sixty times Round the Garden in Twenty Seven Minutes should not go unrecognised.

It was time he wrote a letter.

Wilmot went up to his room after tea.

"I'm just going to do my reading, Mum," he said.

"Oh, right you are, Wilmot," she said surprised, as usually she had to nag him into reading his school book, even when it was a good one.

But reading was just a pretence. It was writing that Wilmot was intent on. He went up to his room and got out his note-pad with the bright orange and yellow paper in it and his pen with the green ink.

People who got letters from Wilmot quite often felt sick, what with all the different colours. The postman didn't like Wilmot's letters all that much either, because he also had a selection of black envelopes. And because Wilmot always addressed his black envelopes in black ink, this made them very difficult to read. His mother had often told him that he should either change to white envelopes or to white ink, one or the other, to make things easier. But Wilmot said that letters were private, and that the postman shouldn't be reading his envelopes anyway. His mum had said that if the postman didn't read his envelopes, how could he ever be expected to deliver them? But Wilmot wasn't having any of that, and he just muttered darkly about nosy postmen and how they ought to mind their own business.

Wilmot had also brought the *World Book of Records* up to his room. He looked up the address of the publisher on the page before the title, found the name of the editor and began to write.

Dear Sir ... Wilmot began, and by the time he had finished, allowing for mis-spellings and crossings out, his letter read like this.

To Mr Peter Matthias,
The Editor,
The World Book of Records,
London.

Dear Sir or Madam,
My name is Wilmot Tanner and I think I have a new record for your books which you can have for £5 – or even for nothing, as long as you promise to put my name in, if that's all right.

It happened like this: I was going all out to beat the one hundred metres record for the world, and my mum was timing me on the oven timer, when due to a misunderstanding,

I went sixty times round the back garden instead. This only took me twenty seven minutes, which I think you'll agree is pretty good going. Especially as I had Mr Ronson to put up with while I was doing it, leaning over the garden fence, and telling me another of his long, boring stories, most of which I think are untrue. In fact, if you are ever looking for the world record holder for long, boring and untrue stories, then Mr Ronson is your man.

But to get to the point, the thing is that I now believe that I have set a new world record for running round our back garden. It is my belief that nobody – and I mean NOBODY – alive or dead, has ever run round our back garden sixty times before, not ever, in the whole history of the universe. Added to this is the other fact that I did it in only twenty seven minutes, and in my trousers.

I think you will agree that this is PRETTY FAST! And I challenge anyone – and I mean ANYONE, including animals, even sharks – but not antelopes, as they have four legs, which would be unfair – to try and get round our garden sixty times in their trousers with Mr Ronson leaning over the fence, in under twenty seven minutes on the oven timer.

I see that you do not have a category in

your record book for running round our back garden, but maybe you would like to create one specially, so that this new record for this new sport – which I'm sure will be of GREAT INTEREST to your readers – can have a place of its own.

Please give this matter your earliest attention, and don't worry too much about the £5. It is the fame that matters to me more than the money, and I am only doing it for the sake of my fans.

Meantime, while waiting to hear from you, I will be making further attempts to set even newer and greater records to fill your pages. I have now set my sights on the World Record for Chips, which I hope one day may even be an Olympic event, like toss the hurdle.

I look forward to your speediest reply in your fastest handwriting at the earliest.

I shall have to close now, as the orange and yellow writing paper and the green ink are making me feel a bit queasy.

Yours
Wilmot Tanner

Wilmot folded up the letter and put it into an envelope – a white one this time, as he wanted to be sure that this letter got there. He scrounged a

stamp from his dad, and left the letter out on the
cabinet next to his bed, so that he would be sure
to remember to take it with him in the morning,
and post it on his way to school.

Then, once he had that out of the way, he could
concentrate on the chips. It was plain that he was
going to need some help in his attempt on the
World Chip Eating Record, and the easiest person
to confide in was Terry. But there were obvious
dangers here. For Terry might think it was a
stupid idea and hold it up to ridicule and scorn.
But on the other hand, he might not, and might
prove to be very helpful.

Wilmot decided to take the risk. He went along
the corridor to Terry's room and politely knocked
on the door.

6

In Training

"**W**ho is it?" Terry said from within.

"Me," said Wilmot.

"What do you want?"

"Talk to you."

"What about?"

"Chips."

There was a moment's hesitation and then, "All right."

Terry told Wilmot to come in and Wilmot explained about the chips. When he had finished, Terry let out a long, low whistle of admiration. "Good idea, Wilmot," he said. "Very good idea."

"Do you think so?" Wilmot said. "Do you really think so?"

"Yes. The world record for the number of chips you can eat in five minutes, pretty good Wilmot, pretty good." Terry looked at Wilmot thoughtfully.

"How many chips do you think you *can* eat in five minutes?"

Wilmot shrugged. "Don't know," he said. "Hundreds, probably."

"Thousands, I should think!" Terry said.

"Not millions, though," Wilmot said, a little anxiously, with visions of his poor stomach, swollen and bloated beyond recognition.

"Or maybe it would be best to weigh them," Terry said.

"How do you mean?"

"Weigh them. Instead of counting them. So instead of getting the record for the number of chips, you make it for the weight of chips! Or you could weigh yourself, before and after, and then take away the difference!"

"Right," said Wilmot, "right." He was pleased that Terry was being so helpful and positive – but he still didn't altogether trust him.

"Of course," Terry said, "you'll have to go into training."

A frown crossed Wilmot's face. "Training?" he said. "How do you mean?"

"Well, you can't expect to go setting world records for eating chips without any training, can you?" Terry said. "You have to do your training. Athletes and everyone, they all have to do their training, don't they? If you want to set any decent sort of a record, you have to train."

Wilmot considered this. Hmm. Yes, he could see that there was some truth in it, but all the same . . .

"But what sort of training though?" he said. "How do you get into training for setting the World Record for Chips?"

Terry sat silently brooding for a while and then he said, "Got it!"

"What?" Wilmot said, excited.

"You go hungry!" Terry said.

"What?" said Wilmot.

"You go hungry," Terry said. "You work up an appetite. In fact you don't eat anything at all for days. So that when it comes to it, you're so hungry and your stomach's so empty, that you can stuff great handfuls of chips down without any trouble at all."

"I don't know about that . . ." Wilmot said. It was the thought of being hungry for days.

"Only way, as far as I can see," Terry said. "Only way to do it if you want to be famous."

"Well, I can't eat *nothing*!" Wilmot objected. "Not *nothing at all*!"

"Okay, well maybe just a few vegetables," Terry said. "But no puddings."

"No puddings?"

"Definitely not puddings."

"But what about Mum?" Wilmot asked. "She won't let me eat nothing. You know what she's like. It's all 'finish your greens' and everything."

"Umm," Terry said. "Look, I've got an idea."

"What?"

"Simple," Terry said. "I'll eat your dinners for you."

"What?"

"Yes. That's what we can do. You can slip your hamburgers or your fish fingers or whatever onto my plate, and give me your ice cream and cakes and puddings and things when Mum's not looking. And in return, so you won't starve to death, I'll give you a few of my vegetables – like my spinach and my cabbage and things."

Wilmot wasn't sure. He could see that Terry was only trying to help him, but all the same, it seemed a little unfair that Terry should get all the nice stuff to eat and that he should be left not only with his own cabbage, but Terry's too.

"I don't know, Ter . . ." he said. The other thing that worried him was that the less he had to eat, the weaker he would become. And in a weakened condition, he might not be able to defend himself. Terry was all right now, but what if he turned nasty again, and sneaked up on Wilmot when he'd had nothing to eat but cabbage for three days and attacked him with a North Korean Arm Lock or something? Wilmot might be too weak by then to fight him off with a Punch in the Coconuts from Fiji.

"Well, it's up to you," Terry said. "I mean, here am I, offering to give up my spinach and all my cabbage and even my broccoli, all for your sake. And here I am, willing to take on the extra work of eating your fish fingers and your puddings and even your chocolate ration . . ."

"My chocolate ration!" Wilmot said.

"Yes, you can't expect to go setting chip records if you're stuffing yourself full of chocolate," Terry cautioned. "And here I am, willing to do all this for you, willing to put my health and my teeth at risk, from eating all these sweet things, Wilmot, just for you . . . and you don't even say thanks."

"Well, it's not that," Wilmot said. "It's not that I'm not grateful . . ."

"Well, I won't offer to help you again," Terry said. "That's all I have to say. Now, if you'll excuse me, I am rather busy with my homework."

"No, no," Wilmot said, "hold on, I didn't say . . ."

Terry's eyes lit up. "It's a deal then?"

"Em, yes, all right, I suppose so. As long as you'll help me with my World Chip Record attempt."

"It's a deal."

44

"Right," Wilmot said, still wondering if he was doing the right thing.

"Starting first thing tomorrow – okay?"

"First thing?" The days of hunger had seemed far away, but suddenly now they seemed all too near.

"Yes. Just to be on the safe side, I'd better eat your breakfast as well."

If Wilmot had been unsure about it the night before, he was even less sure about it the next morning as he sat at the breakfast table, watching Terry eat his cornflakes. Terry had quickly finished his own cereal and as soon as Mum had left the room he had said, "Okay, pass them over," and he had taken Wilmot's full bowl, exchanging it for his own empty one.

Wilmot watched every mouthful, as the spoonfuls of his own breakfast disappeared into Terry's jaws. His stomach gurgled, and pangs of hunger nipped his stomach. It was on the tip of his tongue to say, "No, I've changed my mind. Give me my cornflakes back!" But then he remembered that he was in training – an athlete in training. It was tough at the top, and you had to be tough if you wanted to be a world class chip eater. And that was how it was. No compromises.

His stomach gurgled again.

"When *do* I get anything to eat?" Wilmot said.

"Later," Terry said. "Which reminds me, on our way to school, you'd better give me your lunch."

"What!" said Wilmot. "Lunch as well?" It was more than flesh and blood could bear. Surely even First Division footballers didn't train this hard. "Don't I get anything?"

"Sure," said Terry reaching over – now that he had finished Wilmot's cornflakes – to help himself to Wilmot's toast. "We'll just rearrange our lunch boxes to make sure that you don't get any of the unhealthy stuff. Lean and strong, Wilmot, that's what you've got to be now. Just look on me as your trainer. In fact, maybe you ought to carry my bags to school as well."

"Do what?" Wilmot wailed.

"Keep you fit," Terry said. "Help you work up an appetite."

"I've already got an appetite," Wilmot said. And his stomach gurgled again. "I can hear it."

"It'll take your mind off it then," Terry said. He chewed away at Wilmot's toast. "Good this toast," he said. "Have you got any more?"

"No," said Wilmot. "It's gone. You've eaten it all." He looked sadly at his plate. The hunger was getting worse. "Do you think I could have the crumbs?" he asked. Terry looked from the crumbs on the plate to Wilmot and back.

"Okay," he said, "I suppose it'll be all right. But not too many, and no butter on them."

"How do you butter crumbs?" Wilmot said.

"Actually, now I think about it," Terry said, "I'd better drink your orange juice as well."

7

Celery Sticks

They said cheerio to Mum and left the house as normal, but once they turned the corner, Terry said they ought to stop and sort out Wilmot's training schedule.

"Here," he said. "This'll do. Put your lunch box here."

They put their lunch boxes down on a wall and Terry opened them up.

"I'm going to eliminate all the unnecessary fat from your diet."

"I don't think I have any fat." Wilmot said. "I'm all skin and bone already."

"Now look at this!" Terry said in a tone of disgust. "Now look at this! Will you just look at what Mum's gone and given you! A packet of crisps! Would you believe it. A packet of crisps, and you in training! That's disgusting. I'd better have that." And he took Wilmot's crisps and put them into his own lunch box, along with the bag Mum had already given him.

"But don't you think that . . ." Wilmot weakly protested.

"No, I don't, Wilmot," Terry said, "I'm afraid I don't. The only thing I think of is you. And your World Record. Now let's see what else we've got here." And he took something wrapped in cling-film from Wilmot's lunch box and examined it.

"I don't believe it!" Terry cried. "I simply do not believe it! Giving food like this to an athlete in training! I simply do not believe it! Will you just look at this, Wilmot, this is just terrible!"

"What? What is it?" Wilmot said.

"It's only a chocolate biscuit, if you please! Only a chocolate biscuit, that's all. Cor, it's a narrow escape you've had there, Wilmot, I don't mind telling you. Why, if I hadn't gone and unwrapped that, there's no telling what would have happened. Why, you might even have gone and eaten it!"

"Yes," Wilmot wistfully agreed, "I would have."

"But never mind, you won't need to now. I'll have that," Terry said. And he put it into his own lunch box, along with his own chocolate biscuit. Wilmot was starting to think that if Terry's lunch box got any fuller, he wouldn't be able to close the lid.

There were two further items in Wilmot's lunch box. Terry inspected them closely.

"What else is there?" Wilmot said.

"Only a cheese sandwich," Terry said, in hurt and angry tones. "She's only gone and given you a rotten cheese sandwich to kill yourself with! No, no. No, no, no. No, I'd better have that." And the cheese sandwich, too, found its way into Terry's lunch box. So there was only one thing left. Terry unwrapped and looked at it.

"What's that then?" Wilmot said.

"Well, it seems to be . . . a stick of celery."

"Oh," Wilmot said. He wasn't keen on celery. He usually didn't eat it when Mum put it into his lunch box. He pretended he had when he got home, but usually he just threw it away.

"Hmm . . . celery . . . I don't know . . ." Terry was musing, ". . . but then again . . . just this once! Okay! Okay, Wilmot, you can have the celery."

"Thanks," Wilmot said.

Terry went to close the lunch boxes, but hesitated. "I'll tell you what, Wilmot, I'll tell you what, seeing it's you, I'll give you my stick of celery as well."

"Oh . . . right . . . thanks," Wilmot said. He tried to sound grateful, but it wasn't easy. Two sticks of celery – it didn't seem like such a great lunch to him.

"You know," Terry was saying, "I think this is going to be a big success. The way we're going on here, Wilmot, you're going to be ready to set the World Chip Record in no more than a couple of days."

"The way I feel right now," Wilmot said, "I'm going to have died of hunger in a couple of days. Or even by this evening."

"Stick with it, Wilmot," Terry said encouragingly, "don't give up now when the end's in sight."

"Is it?" Wilmot said. "I can't see it."

"Okay, we'd better get to school or we'll be late. Here you are, Wilmot, you can carry the lunch boxes and the bags – get yourself in trim."

"And what are you going to carry?" Wilmot wanted to know.

"I'm going to carry this big heavy *Beano*," Terry said, "and read it as we go along, so as to try and take my mind off this enormous lunch I'm going to have to eat this afternoon. And I hope you do appreciate, Wilmot, that I'm doing it all . . . for your sake."

"Thanks," said Wilmot. "I'm grateful." And his stomach rumbled like it was having an earthquake.

"It might be best," Terry said, "if you jogged with those bags."

"Jogged?" said Wilmot. "I've hardly got the strength to walk."

"Do you want to be famous or don't you, Wilmot? Do you want to set this World Chip Record or do you not?"

"All right," said Wilmot. "I suppose so. I'll see you there then."

"See you there," said Terry.

So Wilmot picked up the bags and lunch boxes and jogged off to school, while Terry followed on at a casual stroll, leisurely reading his *Beano*.

Sometimes, Terry thought, it was nice to have a brother.

On the way to school, Wilmot remembered to post his letter, though even the effort of reaching up and putting it into the post box taxed his undernourished strength. If this was what he felt like after just not having breakfast, how was he going to feel later on in the day?

When the whistle blew in the playground and they went off to their different class rooms, it was with great longings and sadness that Wilmot watched Terry disappear with his lunch box. It was so packed full of food that he could barely close the lid, while Wilmot's own lunch box rattled emptily with just the two sticks of celery.

The morning passed at a snail's pace. Wilmot tried to listen to what the teacher was saying, but thoughts of food intruded at every turn. His stomach began to gurgle so loudly that Mr Stevens even interrupted the lesson to ask if he was all right.

"Is your stomach making that noise, Wilmot?" he said. "Or is it your head?"

"Sorry," Wilmot apologised. "It's my stomach. I can't seem to control it. It's got a mind of its own."

"Well, I'm glad to hear that your stomach has a mind then, Wilmot, even if your brain does seem a bit short of one on occasion. An extra mind always comes in handy – especially with the difficult sums."

Mr Stevens then wrote some difficult sums on the blackboard for Wilmot's stomach to do. But his stomach didn't seem interested. All it wanted to talk about was food. Even thinking of the fame and fortune ahead couldn't take Wilmot's mind off his stomach, or his stomach's mind off food. Not even the idea of being the World Chip Record Holder made any difference to his hunger. All that Wilmot could really think of was how long till lunch. And the funny thing was that the two sticks of celery – and normally he disliked celery – began to seem as tempting as chocolate. And the way he looked forward to eating the two sticks of celery, they could have been Mars Bars.

By eleven o'clock, Wilmot had stopped being Wilmot, for his stomach was taking him over. By eleven fifteen, Wilmot was half boy, half stomach. By eleven thirty, he was nothing but a stomach and the rest of him had gone. He sat there in the class. A class which no longer consisted of thirty pupils, but which now comprised twenty nine pupils – fifteen girls, and fourteen boys, and Wilmot, the human stomach.

Wilmot wondered why Mr Stevens couldn't see what was happening to him. He wondered that Mr Stevens didn't stop the lesson, and throw his hands up in the air and shout, "Who let that stomach in here? What's that stomach doing in my class? I'm not having any big empty stomachs coming in here, interrupting my lessons."

But he didn't seem to notice. Nobody did. But it was an awful feeling. It reminded Wilmot of the time he had once desperately wanted to go to the loo, and he had turned into a human bladder, and the time he had caught his hand in the door and had turned into a human throbbing thumb.

There was only one thing that mattered now. There was one answer to all questions. And that answer was to be found in his lunch box.

Finally, lunch time came.

"Quick," Wilmot's stomach said. "Food! And masses of it!"

Wilmot got his lunch box and hurried along with the others to the dining hall. He sat down next to Martin Fields, opened his lunch box and took out his celery.

Crunch!

Martin took a huge peanut butter sandwich out of his own lunch box and looked at it with admiration.

Crunch!

"What's that you've got, Wilmot?"

"Celery."

"Eeech! Is that all you're having then?"

Crunch!

"Yes," Wilmot said.

"What for?" Martin said. "You're not slimming, are you? You don't want to get any skinnier, Wilmot, or you'll drop down a drain."

But Wilmot just crunched. Crunch!

"Cor, you ate that quick," Martin said.

Wilmot unwrapped the second stick of celery.

"Of course I'm not on a diet," he said. "I'm in training."

"For what?"

Wilmot decided to tell Martin his plans.

"I'm in training," he said, and then he paused for effect, "for the World Record for Chips!"

If Wilmot had expected a few gasps of admiration from Martin at this announcement, he didn't get them. All he got was a blank look and, "What's that then?"

"I'm going to be in the record books," Wilmot said. "And that's how I'm going to do it, by setting a world record for the number of chips eaten in five minutes. I shall probably do it this weekend, maybe Saturday afternoon. You can be the timekeeper, if you like."

"But what's that got to do with celery?" Martin asked. He had by now eaten his peanut butter sandwich and was unwrapping a Wagon Wheel. Wilmot's stomach saw it and gave a little groan. You wouldn't think that stomachs had eyes, but his did, it saw everything.

"I'm eating as little as possible, so as to be as hungry as I can for the weekend. That way, by having an empty stomach, I'll be raring to eat all the chips, and I'll have plenty of space to put them in. I'll set a record that'll be unbeatable. It'll stand for years!"

Crunch! He bit into his celery again. There was no doubt, it was horrible.

Martin chewed thoughtfully on his Wagon Wheel.

"Who told you that?" Martin said. "About the training?"

"My brother." And Wilmot looked across the hall to a far table, where Terry was sitting laughing and joking with his cronies, while tucking into his second bag of crisps – that were Wilmot's by rights.

"Your brother?" Martin said. "And so you gave him your lunch, did you?"

"Yes," Wilmot said. "He said he'd eat it for me, as a favour. Just to help me out. He said he wouldn't do it for anybody."

"And he gave you his celery?"

"Yes. He said it would be all right to have celery. Very good for athletes in training. In fact, he very kindly ate my breakfast as well. And I dare say he'll have my dinner, too, when we get home. You have to admit, it's pretty decent of him. Because normally we just fight and argue. But this time, he's really turned up trumps."

"Hmm," Martin said, biting another bit of his Wagon Wheel. "And how long does that go on? Your brother eating all your meals, and you having all the horrible stuff he doesn't like?"

"Till the weekend, I suppose," Wilmot said. His stomach gurgled again. Perhaps he should eat the celery slower, to make it last.

"Well," Martin said, not liking to see Wilmot the victim of trickery, "I don't want to cast aspersions on your brother – whatever aspersions are – but it seems to me that he's conned you again, good and proper."

Wilmot's stomach seemed even emptier.

"What do you mean?" he said, his voice hollow.

"I mean," said Martin, "that when you go into training, you practise for the real thing, you practise what you're going to do. So if you go into training for running – well, you run. If you go into training for the high jump – you jump. So it stands to reason that if you're going into training to eat chips, then what you should be doing is eating chips! Lots of them! As many as you can!"

Cru . . .

Wilmot stopped in mid-crunch.

It was true. Martin was right. That *was* what you did. Exactly what you did. If you wanted to get better at something, then you practised it, repeated it, you kept on doing it, over and over again, until you had it right.

. . . nch!

Wilmot bit angrily into the celery. He looked over at Terry in the far corner again. Terry was now wolfing down his second biscuit. Wilmot's biscuit! *Wilmot's* biscuit!

Yes, there was no doubt, Terry had done the dirty on him. He had conned him, good and proper, and Wilmot had gone along with it, as meek as a lamb.

But he would be revenged.

His instinct was to stride across the dining hall and take the biscuit from Terry's hand. But no. Best not to say or do anything yet. Best to wait for his opportunity and to bide his time.

Crunch! Two bites left. But that was it. No more celery then, just bags of chips all the way. Yes, that was the training schedule now. Chips, chips and chips again. Crunch!

And then the record.

And somewhere along the way – revenge.

Crunch!

8

Mrs Wilkins and Mr Chang

The rest of the day passed with endless rumblings of hunger coming from Wilmot's stomach. As soon as the bell rang for the end of school, Wilmot had but one thought in his mind. And that, combined with the fifty pence pocket money in his pocket, meant chips.

And chips meant Chang's Chippy – for the Crispiest Chips this Side of China. Wilmot went there straight from school, his legs going as fast as they could, and his stomach telling them to go even faster.

The door clanged open and the bell above it rang. Mr Chang looked up from the chip cooker.

"Hello, Wilmot," he said. "How are you?"

"Fine," said Wilmot. "How are you?"

"Fine," said Mr Chang. "What do you want?"

"Chips, please," Wilmot said. "Fifty pence worth."

"Okay. You'll have to wait a minute. I've only just put them in. You're early."

Wilmot knew he was early, and he had got there early on purpose, hoping to have a word in private with Mr Chang about a matter of interest to them both, without being disturbed by other customers – or by Mrs Chang. Mrs Chang was only four foot eleven, but she seemed to dominate the shop and to frighten all the customers. She also seemed to frighten Mr Chang, who always went very quiet, and stared at the television whenever she came in, even when it wasn't on.

It had occurred to Wilmot, while talking to Martin during the afternoon break, that a World Chip Record attempt could prove rather expensive. It was a simple matter of finance.

"How are you going to pay for them?" Martin had said.

"What?" Wilmot asked.

"For all the chips you're going to eat in this five minutes. Who's going to pay for them? How many do you think you'll need?"

"Well," Wilmot said, "I'm sure I can eat a bag a minute at least. Maybe two."

"So there you are then," Martin said. "Five minutes of chip eating at two bags a minute, well, that's ten bags of chips minimum, isn't it? And you ought to have another couple of bags for emergencies. So just say twelve. So twelve bags of chips say, at fifty pence a bag, that's ..."

But Wilmot was already working it out on a piece of paper.

"Six pounds," he said, his face falling with dismay. Where was he going to get that kind of money? "Six pounds! That's a fortune! I'll have to call my attempt on the World Chip Record off."

"Maybe not though," Martin said. "What you need is a sponsor. Like somebody with their own chip shop, maybe."

"That's it," said Wilmot. "Yes, that's it. Martin, you're like me – you're a genius!"

Mr Chang put the television on, then promptly ignored it, and began to read his newspaper, while waiting for the chips to cook. Wilmot didn't know quite how to start the conversation he wanted to have, so he coughed and cleared his throat to get Mr Chang's attention.

Mr Chang looked up. "You got a cold, Wilmot?" he said. "Because if you have, can you go and cough outside. I don't want any germs on my chips."

"No, no," Wilmot said, "I just wanted to ask ... wondered, that is ... if you'd be interested at all in ... a business proposition, Mr Chang."

Mr Chang turned a page of his paper.

"Business proposition?" he said, peering doubtfully at Wilmot. "With you?"

"I believe, Mr Chang," Wilmot said, "that I can put your chip shop on the map!"

"It's already on the map," Mr Chang said, and he took out a battered and chip-stained A-Z from under the counter. He opened it at a page and showed it to Wilmot. "There you are, you see," he said. "West Grove Road, and that's my shop there!" And he pointed to a blue ink mark next to which was written 'My chip shop'.

"No, that wasn't quite what I meant," Wilmot said. "I meant that I could make your chip shop famous. Your name would be in all the papers!"

"My name already is in the papers," Mr Chang said. "It's on all the chip papers."

"I mean the newspapers," Wilmot said. "You see, I am soon going to be undertaking certain chip related activities, Mr Chang, and I shall probably need a sponsor."

Mr Chang looked at him dubiously, "Chip related activities?" he said. "Sponsor? What do you mean?"

"A sponsor like at the football," Wilmot said.

"I don't cook footballs," Mr Chang said. "I use nothing but the finest ingredients. Who's been spreading these rumours that my meals are made out of footballs? I'll have the law on to them!"

"No, no," Wilmot said, "I mean on their shirts!"

"I don't cook shirts either," Mr Chang said. "Who says I've been cooking shirts? I'll sue them for slander!"

"No, what I mean, Mr Chang, is that sometimes businessmen, like yourself, put money into football teams, and become their sponsors. And when they do, the football teams wear shirts with the sponsors' names on them. So the businessmen become famous, and everyone sees their names on TV."

"Ah, right," Mr Chang nodded. "Yes, sure, I've seen them. So?"

"Well, what I was thinking," Wilmot said, "was that maybe you and I could come to a similar arrangement, Mr Chang, and I could wear your shirt."

"You want to wear my shirt?" Mr Chang said. "But it's too big for you. And besides, what would I wear? And what would your mother say? And worse ... " and his voice dropped to a whisper, " ... what would Mrs Chang say?"

"No, Mr Chang, no, I don't want to actually wear your shirt," Wilmot explained, feeling that he wasn't putting things very well. "I meant that I could wear my own shirt, but it would have your name on it."

"Ah, right," Mr Chang said. "Right. So you want me to write my name on your shirt?"

"Yes!"

"Yes? Okay, no trouble. I'll just get a biro."

"No, I mean, not right now! Not just at the moment."

"Okay. Well, call round any time, Wilmot. Any time you want me to write my name on your shirt, you just call round, and as long as I'm not too busy, I'll be happy to do that for you."

It wasn't going well, Wilmot thought. It was always happening to him and he didn't know why. Other people seemed to manage all right. They seemed to get through life without these problems. But for him, muddle and misunderstandings seemed to blossom like weeds. And even the simplest thing, like asking Mr Chang to sponsor him in his attempt on the World Chip Record was fraught with complications.

One more try. One more, and if that didn't work, Wilmot thought, then he would just have to go off somewhere quietly and shoot himself.

"The thing is, Mr Chang ... "

"Hmm?" Mr Chang said, by now back reading his paper.

"I'm going to make an attempt on the World

Chip Record, and I wondered if you would care to sponsor me?"

Mr Chang looked up. He folded his paper and put it away under the counter. Wilmot had his interest now, and his attention.

"The World Chip Record?" he said. "You mean someone's made a record? With chips? You mean, singing chips? Like in squeaky voices? Like the Muppets?"

"No, I mean, Mr Chang, that I am going to get into the record books by eating the most chips ever in five minutes. Only I might not have enough money to buy all the chips I'll need. So I wondered if you would like to sponsor me by *giving* me the chips, and then, while I was making an attempt on the record – which I could even do here, in your chip shop if you like – I could wear a T-shirt with *Chang's Chips* on the front, and *Eat At Chang's* on the back. So then, when the newspapers and the television came round, you'd get lots of publicity. And soon your chips would be famous the world over. And then you could open new chip shops all over the place! And you'd be a millionaire."

Mr Chang took a wire basket of golden chips out of the cooker and dumped them into the display part of the cabinet, ready to be dished out.

"Let me get this right," he said. "You want to see how many chips you can eat in five minutes?"

"Right!" Wilmot said. They were getting somewhere now.

"And you want me to give them to you?"

"Right!" Wilmot agreed. That was it.

"For nothing?" Mr Chang said.

"Right!" Wilmot said.

"And in return for the free chips, you will wear a T-shirt with Chang's Chips on it?"

"Right!"

"Who pays for the T-shirt?" Mr Chang said, his voice not quite so friendly.

"Em ... you do, Mr Chang. That's part of the sponsorship deal – providing the kit."

"I see. So you get free chips and you get a nice free T-shirt ... and what do I get again?"

"Fame and fortune, Mr Chang. So what do you say?"

"No," said Mr Chang. "That's what I say. No." And he wrapped up Wilmot's order. "Here's your chips, Wilmot," he said. "That's fifty pence."

Wilmot paid for the chips. He shook salt and vinegar over them and headed for the door.

"Sure you don't want to change your mind, Mr Chang?"

"No thank you, Wilmot, but good luck."

Wilmot was half inclined to stay and see if he

couldn't persuade Mr Chang to change his mind. But then Mrs Chang appeared behind the counter, and she muttered something in Chinese to Mr Chang, which Wilmot could not understand, but which sounded very much to him like, "What does spotty face want?"

To which Mr Chang replied, also in Chinese, "Free chips and a T-shirt!"

To which Mrs Chang said, "He'll be lucky!"

And at that, Wilmot decided it was time to go.

Disappointed, but feeling better for the chips, Wilmot walked towards home. His stomach wasn't nagging him so much, now that it had something to work on. And he still had his revenge on Terry to occupy his mind. It would be a shame, though, if he had to abandon his World Chip Record attempt, just for lack of a sponsor.

The World Chip Record had seemed just right for him. Some records didn't really amount to much – things like how far along the road you could push a pea with your nose, and stuff like that. But the World Chip Record had a certain style, a certain ring to it, a certain ...

Wilmot stopped in his tracks.

All was not yet lost.

How could he have forgotten? Chang's wasn't the only chip shop in the neighbourhood. There was Wilkins's too. Wilkins's Traditional Chip

Shop. Chips Like Your Mother Used To Make, the sign said. Only somebody had vandalised the sign with a spray can and altered it to Chips Like Your Mother Used To Burn.

Wilkins's trade had been badly hit by the arrival of Chang's Chip Shop, and it was hardly surprising. The quality of Wilkins's chips had gone down over the years, for the truth was that Mrs Wilkins was no longer really up to it. She and her husband had once run the chip shop together and the place had thrived, but since he had died, she had lost interest in the business, and trade had got steadily worse.

Wilmot finished the chips he was eating, and put the paper into a bin. He took a deep breath, checked his appearance in the dusty shop window, and went into Wilkins's Chip Shop.

Chang's Chip Shop had been bright and welcoming, but Wilkins's Chip Shop was dark and gloomy by comparison. Chang's also had a large menu with thirty or forty different dishes to choose from, but Wilkins's only had fish, chips, saveloys, mushy peas, pickled onions and bread and butter.

Mrs Wilkins was at the sink behind the counter, cutting up potatoes, up to her elbows in peelings.

"Hello, Wilmot," she said. "Haven't seen you

lately. I expect you've been getting your chips at Chang's, same as the rest of them."

"No, Mrs Wilkins, not me," he lied, feeling a pang of guilt and disloyalty. For Mrs Wilkins had always been kind to him when he was a baby. And she often used to give him a free chip, or a pickled onion to play with.

"How's your mum?" Mrs Wilkins said.

"Fine thanks," Wilmot said.

"Do you want a fish supper?" Mrs Wilkins said. "Because they won't be ready for a while yet. I've only just started to peel the potatoes."

"But can't you get a machine to do all that?" Wilmot said. "Or even buy your chips ready peeled?"

"Don't hold with it," Mrs Wilkins said. "Not these new methods. Traditional chips it says above the door, and traditional chips it is, rain or shine."

"No, I haven't actually come in for chips," Wilmot said.

"Doesn't surprise me," Mrs Wilkins said. "Nobody ever does these days."

"No, the reason I've called ... " Wilmot began, and he went on to outline his sponsorship scheme to Mrs Wilkins in as few words as possible. And he explained how if she gave him all the chips he could eat in five minutes he would make her rich and famous.

"Not much point in being rich and famous at my age, dear," she said. "I've left it all a bit too late."

That was it then. No joy. Wilmot sighed inwardly. He would just have to find another record to beat.

"But all right then, if you like."

"Okay, Mrs Wilkins, well, thanks anyway. I hope you didn't mind my asking," and he headed for the door. He stopped. Just a minute. What had she said? Had she actually said ... yes?

"Yes, I'm closing down the business on Saturday," Mrs Wilkins said. "I'm selling up and going to live with my sister who's retired to the Isle of Wight. She used to be a belly dancer, but she got too thin and her belly disappeared. But it would make a nice send-off, to have the World Chip Record established in my chip shop and with my chips. And it would use up the last of the potatoes as well. All right then, Wilmot, you're on."

Wilmot left the shop walking on air. He couldn't believe his good luck. But that was how it went. Sometimes you felt as if the world was against you, and the only word you ever heard was, "No!" But then, out of the blue, along came someone who actually said, "Yes!" And the sun shone again.

And there were rainbows everywhere. And the lightness was back in your step.

To add to his joy, Wilmot had also thought of a suitable revenge for Terry. 'Payment in kind' were the words which went through his mind. Yes, payment in kind. He hurried home, for if he left it too late, his chance for revenge would have gone. Terry – in fact his whole family – were creatures of habit, and Wilmot's revenge depended on their doing as they always did on a Tuesday night. One thing he couldn't afford to do was to disrupt the usual routine.

He hurried on then, and arrived back with minutes to spare. Five minutes to tea time. Absolutely perfect.

He was cool and icy calm as he entered the kitchen. He knew exactly what he had to do.

First, he was going to eat his dinner.

And then he was going to eat Terry's dinner as well.

And then he was going to give him a Mongolian Smack in the Pineapples.

9

Payment in Kind

Everything looked ordinary. That was good. You wanted things to look normal when you were up to something.

Mum was in the kitchen, cooking spaghetti. Tuesday night was always spaghetti night, for reasons that nobody knew. It hadn't always been spaghetti night, Wilmot supposed, like back when he was a really small baby. He must have eaten other things then, like fruit puree and rusks. But Tuesday had been spaghetti night ever since his memory had first started working. And the first maths sum he had learnt was that Tuesday + dinner = spaghetti.

It was real spaghetti that Mum was cooking. Not the stuff in tins, with the sauce already on it, but real long spaghetti, from a blue packet, and she made her own sauce for it, and it was delicious. And despite the chips he had just had, Wilmot was still starving.

Two places were set at the table, one for him and one for Terry. Mum would eat later with Dad, when he got home. Terry was nowhere to be seen, but Wilmot knew that he would be up in his room listening to his radio. There was a programme which he always listened to on Tuesday and which finished at five o'clock. There was also a television programme starting at five o'clock which Mum liked to watch. So at three minutes to five she would fill two tumblers with orange juice, dish out the spaghetti and say to Wilmot, "Wilmot – tea's ready. Would you give Terry a shout while I go and watch my programme?"

And Wilmot would say, "Okay!"

Then Mum would go through to the sitting room to watch her programme, and Wilmot would give Terry a call, saying something like, "Hey, fathead! Your tea's ready!" or "Oi! Slob features, your spaghetti's getting cold!"

On hearing this, Terry would then shout back, "In a minute, freak-face, when my programme's finished!" And he would hear the end of his programme in his room before galumphing down the stairs at five o'clock like a famished elephant.

But tonight, when Mum said, "Give Terry a shout, Wilmot, I'm going to watch my programme," this time, Wilmot just sat down at the table and he started on the spaghetti alone.

Wilmot's stomach was cheering up by now, and was more like its usual self. After having endured half a day of deprivation and celery, it had then been unexpectedly consoled by a surprise bag of chips, and was now getting a nice plateful of spaghetti put into it, to keep the chips company.

This was more like it. This was what a stomach liked.

Wilmot wound the spaghetti round his fork and put it into his mouth. He was quite an expert at spaghetti by now. Gone were the days when he used to splatter the sauce all over himself and half way up the walls. Now he could eat a whole plateful of the stuff without dropping more than one or two forkfuls down his trousers.

It was surprising how hungry he was, even despite the chips. Martin must have been right. The more you eat, the bigger your stomach gets, and the more room there is in it for even more food.

One more mouthful and his plate would be empty. Wilmot looked up at the kitchen clock. Five past five. Not bad. A whole plate of spaghetti in five minutes. Maybe once he'd set the World Chip Record, he'd have a go at the World Spaghetti Record. He could end up as an all-round athlete.

The last forkful slipped down as easily as the first. Wilmot pushed the empty plate away from him and reaching over he drew Terry's full plate towards him, together with Terry's clean knife and fork. Then he set his empty plate in Terry's place. He took up the clean fork, dug deep with it into the mound of pasta, twisted it round to gather the spaghetti up and began to eat Terry's dinner.

Up in his room, Terry was starting to wonder when he would get the call for dinner. His radio programme had finished, so it had definitely gone five o'clock, and dinner was usually spot on five on a Tuesday, but tonight there seemed to be some delay. So he re-tuned his radio to another station, and lay on his bed listening and waiting for the sound of Wilmot, the human dinner gong.

Terry could easily have gone downstairs, of course, and just asked where the dinner was. And he would have caught Wilmot in the act of scoffing his spaghetti. But something stopped him. Habit, maybe. Pride, perhaps. Going down and asking wasn't really, well ... cool.

It wasn't how things were done. Every Tuesday at five, Wilmot got sent up to tell him that dinner was ready. He did it reluctantly, Terry knew, and only because Mum had asked him. But it was still his job to do it.

So it wasn't really for Terry to go downstairs

and ask where dinner was, that would have been a loss of face and a loss of his status and his privileges as an elder brother. No, it was Wilmot's job to come up and get him. Terry had seniority, after all.

Only where was Wilmot? He was taking his time.

Wilmot wasn't taking his time with the spaghetti though, he was wolfing it down. Three more forkfuls and the second plateful would have gone the way of the first. Wilmot's stomach wasn't quite so sure about spaghetti now, but it kept on coming down the hatch, like fish dropping into a trawler.

Last one. Wilmot got the last forkful down. The clock read five fourteen. Mum wouldn't be back for sixteen minutes. So he had done the spaghetti. Now it was time to eat Terry's pudding.

He went to the fridge, took out the two bowls of chocolate whip that Mum had left for them, and brought them to the table. Wilmot took Terry's bowl and upturned it into his own. Then he picked up his spoon and began to eat.

Terry looked at his bedside clock. Dinner *was* late tonight. Very late. Service was getting terrible in this establishment. The two lunches he had eaten – his own, and the one he had tricked Wilmot into handing over – had filled him up good and proper for a while, but even they were starting to wear off now. He was a growing boy, after all, and a growing boy needs his grub.

Only where was the grub? If Wilmot didn't come up and get him soon, he would have to go down and investigate. He could pretend to have gone down about something else, and then he could casually mention dinner as an afterthought.

Yes, that should do it – the casual approach. He'd leave it another ten minutes, and then he'd wander down with his hands in his pockets, maybe yawning a bit and scratching himself. No sense in seeming too eager. He didn't want people thinking that he actually ever got hungry.

Wilmot spooned the last of the chocolate whip down.

It had been a funny old day, his stomach was thinking, very changeable weather. It had started off badly, got worse, but then round about four in the afternoon, it had taken a turn for the better when there had been a nice refreshing downpour of chips, followed by an outbreak of scattered spaghetti, and now it was snowing chocolate whip. Very satisfactory.

Wilmot let out a contented sigh. All done. Delicious. He sat back in his seat. It was all right this training. If this was all there was to keeping fit – eating double spaghetti and chocolate whip, and then sitting back in your chair with your trousers undone – then he was a natural born athlete. That World Chip Record was going to be his, easy as peasy.

He heard the sitting room door open. Mum's TV programme must have finished. In a moment of panic, Wilmot looked across the table and saw that Terry's dessert spoon was clean and unused. It was a giveaway. If Mum saw that, she'd know at once that Wilmot had eaten Terry's pudding.

Footsteps came along the corridor. Wilmot grabbed Terry's spoon, licked it to smear it with chocolate, and threw it back into Terry's bowl with a clatter, just as Mum opened the door.

"Everything okay?" Mum said.

"Fine, thanks. Delicious," Wilmot said.

"Enjoy the spaghetti?"

"Lovely," Wilmot said. "I could have eaten two platefuls!"

"And the chocolate whip?"

"I could have eaten double helpings."

"Where's Terry?"

"Oh, up in his room, I'd imagine," Wilmot said, all innocence.

"I wish he wouldn't do that," Mum said. "Go dashing off up to his room like that, the instant he's finished, without even putting his bowl in the sink."

"Here," said Wilmot, "I'll help you."

"Thank you, Wilmot," Mum said. "Just put it all in the basin."

Wilmot stood up to help and his trousers fell down.

"Why are your trousers round your knees, Wilmot?" Mum said. "And don't tell me it's a project for homework, like you usually do."

"No, I just undid them a bit," Wilmot said. "They felt a bit tight after the spaghetti."

"Oh, okay. Well, go up and do your homework, and then have a bath or a shower. And would you tell Terry to do the same. I want to put your clothes in the wash."

"Okay, Mum, all right," he said, and he headed for the door. "And by the way – lovely tea!"

It was nice to have your cooking appreciated, Mum thought. It made it all worth the effort.

10

Swiss Army Elbow

Half past? No, it was twenty five to. And Terry's stomach bore a puzzled expression. Dinner, it asked, where was it?

Terry turned his radio off and swung his legs off the bed. He made his way casually to the bedroom door, opened it, and stepped out on to the landing just in time to see Wilmot climbing heavily up the stairs.

Terry feigned nonchalance as they passed.

"Hello, Ter," Wilmot said.

"Oh," said Terry. "Wilmot! It's you!" He said it as though after living all these years in the same house as his brother, he was still surprised to see him walking around the place.

"Yes," said Wilmot. "It is. I'm going to have a

bath. And Mum says you've got to have one early too. She wants your clothes for the wash."

Just a minute, Terry thought. This was strange. Have a bath *before* dinner? That couldn't be right.

"Oh, I'll just go downstairs first," Terry said in an off-hand way. "Better see about some dinner, I suppose. I expect it'll be spaghetti *again*, seeing it's Tuesday. Still, better make the effort to eat it. Or Mum'll only get upset and think we don't like her cooking." Terry made a long-suffering face. "Things I do," he said, "for other people."

"No, it's all right, Terry," Wilmot said, pushing past him to get to the bathroom. "You don't have to bother, I've saved you the trouble."

Terry froze. He looked at his brother.

"What do you mean?" he said, his voice a croak.

"I mean," said Wilmot, "that I've eaten your dinner for you."

"Oh, that's all right then, thanks, Wilmot. Because you know, just for a moment there, I thought you said ... " He stared at Wilmot. "It was what you said! You've eaten my what?"

"Your dinner," Wilmot said, "and very nice it was too. Spaghetti and chocolate whip. It went down a treat. You really enjoyed it."

Terry didn't say anything for a while. And then he said, "You are joking, aren't you?"

But Wilmot had to say that no, he wasn't.

They just stood there, looking at each other. Terry wondering what he should do, and Wilmot also wondering what Terry would do, and what he could do to stop it. And then Terry said.

"Have you made a will, Wilmot?"

"A will?" said Wilmot. "What's that?"

"It's a sort of letter," Terry said, "that you write, saying what you want to happen to all your belongings when you die, and who you want to leave them to."

"No," said Wilmot, "I haven't made a will. Why do you ask? I'm not going to die, am I?"

"Yes, you are," said Terry, "and very soon. Because I'm going to kill you!"

"Me?" Wilmot said. "What for?"

"For eating my dinner!"

"Ah, but you ate my lunch. And my breakfast. All I had all day were two sticks of celery!"

"I was helping you," Terry said, "with your training!"

"You were conning me with your lying fibs again!" Wilmot said. "People don't train by starving themselves to death. That's not how you train for anything. You told me porkies."

"My training methods just happen to be a bit different, that's all!" Terry said.

"Your training methods are a load of rubbish," Wilmot said.

"I'm starving!" Terry said. "I won't get anything now until breakfast!"

"You can always chew your fingernails," Wilmot said. "Lots of nourishment in fingernails. Why, I know of lots of top athletes who've won gold medals, and all they ate for years were fingernails!"

"I'm going to tell Mum what you've done," Terry said. "I'm going to tell her that you pinched my dinner!" And he turned to go down the stairs.

"You do that," Wilmot warned, "and I'll tell her that you ate my lunch!"

Terry turned back. No, he couldn't tell Mum then, that was true enough. He would have to sort this out on his own.

"In that case, Wilmot," he said, "I'm afraid that I'm just going to have to give you an Italian Poke in the Spaghetti."

And he did.

For a moment, Wilmot thought he was going to be seriously ill. But the feeling soon passed, and he retaliated with a Maltese Mule Hoof. But Terry was ready for this though, and he blocked it with a Swiss Army Elbow, and followed through with a Spanish Throttle with Extra Tight Guitar Strings, which soon had Wilmot's eyeballs all but bulging out of his head.

Wilmot feared he was a gonner, and wondered

if he should have made a will after all. But then, at the last moment, he saw his opportunity and caught Terry unawares with a Boot up the Bottom from Botswana, which had him crashing into the wall so that he was soon seeing Stars with Extra Twinkle.

But it wasn't over yet. Terry picked himself up off the floor, and came at Wilmot with what looked like a perfectly ordinary Hungarian Head Hammer, which Wilmot went to deflect with an Algerian Aside. But just as he got near, Terry cleverly turned the Hungarian Head Hammer into a Road Drill with Double Rhino Horns from Rangoon, which took Wilmot completely unawares, and he fell to the floor in pain.

They tussled for a few seconds, but Wilmot's dinners had slowed him down, whereas Terry's hunger lent keenness to his fighting.

Terry managed to get on top of Wilmot then and to hold down both his arms. He threatened to finish him off with a Danish Dribble in the Eye from Copenhagen, but Wilmot kicked out and flipped Terry over so that he was on top instead. He sat on Terry's head and was just about to suffocate him with an evil-smelling Cosmic Wind with Intergalactic Cabbages when Terry bucked and threw him off. Terry went in for the kill immediately, with a Turkish Toe Hold on the Half

Ankle. Wilmot writhed and struggled to free himself, and he went to give Terry an Ethiopian Ear
Twist with Double Short and Curlies when a
shadow loomed above both of them and a voice
said, "And just what do you two think you're
doing?"

It was Mum.

She gave them a Long Ticking Off, then, with
Extra Lectures, and said that if they didn't both
stop all this squabbling and go and have a bath
at once, she'd give them both a No Pocket Money
Week, followed by a No TV for a Fortnight.

At that they stopped fighting and slunk off into
the bathroom.

They were too big to have a bath together any
more, for they made the water slop over the sides,
and Terry's toe would be up Wilmot's nose, and
Wilmot's foot would be in Terry's ear. So Wilmot
went to have a shower, in the separate shower
cubicle, while Terry ran a bath.

"I'll get you," hissed Terry, so that Mum
wouldn't hear. "I'm going to write this down in my
Grudge Book and underline it in red ink – twice."

"Only doing what you did to me!" Wilmot hissed
back.

"I'm starving now, I am," Terry said. "I'll be
starving all night and I won't get anything till
breakfast, thanks to you. I may even have to eat

this bath sponge and have my face cloth for afters."

"Serves you right!" Wilmot said. But he felt sorry for Terry. It wasn't nice to be hungry, as he knew. And it wouldn't be very pleasant to be hungry all night, and to keep waking up with hunger pangs, and to go putting your light on, and looking at the clock, and wondering how long till breakfast.

"I'll probably die," Terry said, "of malnutrition. I'll be on the News tomorrow. I'll be in the record books myself. I'll hold the record for being dead."

"All right," said Wilmot, "I'll get you something. But let it be a lesson to you, not to go pulling one over on me again."

"All right," said Terry.

"Friends then?" said Wilmot.

"Okay, then," Terry said. "Friends – if you can get me something to eat."

"Okay," said Wilmot, "in a minute."

He finished his shower, put on his pyjamas, and took his clothes downstairs for the wash.

What could he get Terry to eat? There was the cat food lying in a bowl, but Terry probably wouldn't want that. He knew that Terry would eat almost anything, but even he probably drew the line at cat food – though you never knew.

He could hear Mum approaching out in the hall,

so he had to be quick. He grabbed what he could – an apple and a banana from the fruit bowl, a bag of peanuts from the cupboard, a small box of raisins and a slice of bread. He stuffed the lot inside his pyjama bottoms and waddled up to the bathroom with it all before Mum could see him.

When he got to the bathroom, Terry was still in the bath.

"Didn't you get me anything?" Terry said, seeing Wilmot enter empty-handed.

"It's all in here," Wilmot said, taking the food out of his pyjama bottoms.

"Honestly," said Terry. "What a place to put my dinner!"

"Well, I had to smuggle it out," Wilmot said.

"Give it here!" He looked at it. "Is this all you could get?"

"Don't have it then, if you don't want it."

"Oh, all right, I suppose."

"Friends then?" Wilmot said.

"All right," Terry said, biting into the apple. "Friends."

Wilmot was glad to hear it. He was pleased that they were friends again. He might need Terry's help, when he made his attempt on Saturday on the World Chip Record.

Saturday wasn't far away, and preparations would have to be made. World record attempts such as this were of national interest and importance.

It might be best if Wilmot alerted the media.

11

Mine's a Wilkins

As things stood, Wilmot had it all at least half organised. He had the venue (Wilkins's Chip Shop), he had the time (Saturday afternoon), he had the sponsor (Mrs Wilkins), he had the chips (Mrs Wilkins again), he had the time-keeper (Martin Fields with his mum's alarm clock), and he had the official witness (Terry, though he hadn't asked him yet), and he had the T-shirt.

No he didn't.

Hang on a minute. He didn't have the T-shirt at all. He couldn't even remember now, had he explained to Mrs Wilkins that he should have a T-shirt with *Wilkins's Chips* on the front of it and *Eat at Wilkins* on the back and *Chips by Wilkins* on the left sleeve and *Sponsored by Wilkins* on the right, or hadn't he?

Maybe he should get a baseball cap, too. One with *Mine's a Wilkins* on the peak. Or maybe that was going too far.

Maybe he'd better ring her up.

Wilmot found the number of the chip shop in the Yellow Pages and rang up Mrs Wilkins from the living room while Mum and Dad were in the kitchen having their tea.

"Hello? Mrs Wilkins?" he said.

"Yes, dear?"

"It's Wilmot."

"Yes, dear?"

"I'm not interrupting you, am I? You're not busy?"

She wasn't – just as he expected she wouldn't be.

"It's about Saturday . . . "

"Oh, yes?" she said. For one awful moment, Wilmot thought that she had forgotten. But she hadn't. "The World Chip Record, Wilmot, yes, I remember."

"The thing is," Wilmot said, "I was wondering if you'd like me to wear a special T-shirt."

"What for?"

"The TV cameras."

"What TV cameras?"

"That is, just in case there are any. For publicity, you know."

"Well, you please yourself, Wilmot," Mrs Wilkins said. "I'll leave it up to you."

"But wouldn't you like me to wear a T-shirt with your name on it, like at the football?" Wilmot said. "To advertise your chips."

"Not much point, is there, when I'm closing the shop? Not much point in advertising my chips, Wilmot, when I'm going to be off in the Isle of Wight, and there won't be any chips for sale."

"Not unless you were thinking of doing mail order," Wilmot said.

"No, dear. I'm not thinking of doing mail order. I don't think mail order chips would ever catch on, somehow. I mean, just think about it, Wilmot. They'd be hot when you posted them, but by the time they got to their destination the next day, they'd be stone cold."

"Could warm them up," Wilmot said. "Pop them in the microwave."

"Not the same, dear, not microwaves. You don't get the flavour. No, I'll leave it up to you, I'm sure," Mrs Wilkins said. "It's your big moment, after all. It's just a way of getting rid of my old potatoes, as far as I'm concerned."

"Well, I have got a T-shirt with a picture of Dumbo on the front. I could always wear that," Wilmot suggested.

"What's Dumbo got to do with chips?" Mrs Wilkins said.

"Not a lot, but it would look nice for the cameras," Wilmot said.

"Okay, dear," Mrs Wilkins said. "As I say, it's all up to you. See you on Saturday, about three o'clock would do. Must ring off. I think I've actually got a customer."

And she hung up.

Right. So that was the T-shirt problem taken care of. There was just the publicity to arrange now, and a bit more training to do, and then it was all down to his performance on the day.

Wilmot wasn't too sure how to go about the publicity angle, so he decided to confer with Martin Fields the next day. He was going to ask Terry at first, but he worried that Terry would only find another way of talking him out of his lunch, so he didn't.

Martin's dad had once worked for a TV shop, delivering televisions in his van, and so Martin was recognised to be a TV and media expert. Wilmot asked him during break time what he should do to get the television cameras round to Mrs Wilkins's Chip Shop on the coming Saturday to cover his World Chip Record attempt. He was sure it was the sort of thing that would interest them.

"So what do you think, Martin?" Wilmot asked. "Who should I ring up?"

"Well, I think you should ring the Desk!" Martin said decisively.

"What Desk?" Wilmot said.

"The News Desk," Martin told him. "When you've got anything of interest that you want to get on TV, you have to ring up the Desk."

Wilmot wasn't so sure. "Are you sure it's news?" he said. "I was wondering if it wasn't more sports? Being on a Saturday afternoon and all."

"Could be," Martin agreed. "Yes, maybe you should ask to speak to the Sports Desk. That would probably be it."

"Right," said Wilmot. "I'll do it when I get home."

The day dragged after that, and Wilmot was impatient to get through it. Then when he got home, it seemed that he would never be left alone to make a phone call to the TV company, whose number he had found in the phone book.

At last he was left alone in the sitting room. He rang the number of the TV station and got through to the switchboard.

"Yes?" said a languid woman's voice at the other end of the phone. "County Television, your local station, first with the news and views. Can I help you?"

"Oh, yes please," said Wilmot. "I'd like to speak to the Desk."

There was a slight pause. Then the woman said, "I see. And whose desk would you like to speak to?"

"Well, the News Desk or the Sports Desk, please," Wilmot said. "Or failing that, whatever you've got. As long as I can speak to one of the Desks, I don't really mind."

"Well, all our Desks are rather busy just now," the woman said. "Unless you wanted the Gardening Desk."

"No thanks," said Wilmot, "not really. Sports or News if you wouldn't mind."

"Ah, Sports is free now," the woman said. "Putting you through."

There was a click and some bleeps, and then another phone was picked up and a man's voice spoke gruffly into the phone.

"Harry Garter speaking," it said.

Wilmot recognised the voice immediately. He had often seen Harry Garter doing the commentaries for the TV sport on a Saturday afternoon, looking windswept as he interviewed footballers on the touch-line.

"Ah . . . " Wilmot said. For a moment his nerve failed him.

"Yes?" Harry said impatiently. He was plainly a busy man.

"The thing is ... " Wilmot said.

"Yes?"

"My name's Wilmot," said Wilmot.

"Oh yes?" Harry said.

"And I'm going for the World Chip Record at Mrs Wilkins's Chip Shop on Saturday afternoon at three, and I wondered if you'd like to send a camera crew down to cover it. And maybe you could do the commentary."

There was a silence. Then Harry spoke. "Chips?" he said. "Chips? World Chip Record?"

"Yes, I'm going to establish it," Wilmot said. "And get into the record books. I'm sure it would make great television. It would really draw in the crowds."

"How old are you?" Harry said. Wilmot didn't really want to answer that, for he knew that in some people's eyes youth counted against you and they stopped taking you seriously.

"I'm ... youngish," Wilmot said. "Why?"

"Listen, matey," Harry said. "This coming Saturday, Rangers are playing Rovers at soccer and the Barbarians are playing the Vikings at rugby. Then Mike Dupree is fighting Elvis 'The Sandbag' Simpson for the heavyweight boxing title, and 'Fast' Lucy Limpet is fighting Mavis 'The Muscles'

Crumple in the women's professional wrestling finals. Now, do you really think, with all that going on, that anyone is going to be interested in watching a spotty boy stuff his face with chips down at Mrs Wilkins's Chip Shop?"

"It was only a suggestion," Wilmot said, hurt. "And I'm not spotty!" He hesitated a moment. "Well, not that spotty."

"Sorry, matey," Harry Garter said. "No can do. This is the big time. We're not interested in small potatoes."

"They're not small potatoes. They're chips!" Wilmot said, feeling that Harry hadn't been listening.

"Tell you what, try the local rag," Harry said. "The Herald. The weekly newspaper. You know, the one they give away free. The one you put straight into your dustbin without reading it. Why don't you try them? They might be interested. Sorry we can't help. Bye." And he hung up.

Well, thought Wilmot. That was it between him and Harry Garter now. He wouldn't be watching his programmes any more. No way.

He looked up the number of the Herald and rang through. A man answered the phone, he sounded rather old and doddery.

"H . . . hello?" he said.

"Hello," said Wilmot. "Can I speak to the Desk?"

"This is the Desk speaking," said the voice.

"Are you the Sports Desk or the News Desk?" Wilmot said.

"All of them," the man said. "And the Features Desk. And just in case you were wondering, I'm the filing cabinets as well."

"I don't really want to speak to the filing cabinets," Wilmot said.

"Just as well," the man told him, "'cause I can't find the key. So what can I do for you?"

Wilmot explained about the World Chip Record and Mrs Wilkins's Chip Shop, and how she was retiring to the Isle of Wight after fifty years in the chip business.

"Oh, that's interesting," the man said. "Local interest that. Local shop keeper moving on after fifty years. Yes, I'll come round and have a word with her. And maybe take a photograph ... if I can find my camera ... and a film."

"Yes, and you won't forget about the World Chip Record, will you?" Wilmot said, feeling that the old man had rather missed the point. It was his world record that was important. Not Mrs Wilkins's retirement.

"Now what time did you say would be convenient? Three o'clock, was it? Saturday afternoon? At the chip shop?"

"That's right," Wilmot said. "I'll be wearing my T-shirt with Dumbo on the front."

"Righty-ho," the man said. "And I'll be wearing my waistcoat with the fag ash on the front and my tie with the tomato ketchup on it – not that I'm proud of it, mind, but I just can't get it off. Now what's your name?"

"Wilmot," said Wilmot. "And yours?"

"Puddley," the man said.

"Pardon?" said Wilmot.

"Puddley," the man said. "Right, well, see you on Saturday, Wilmot. Three o'clock."

"Right," said Wilmot, "and you won't forget that the important story is my World . . . " But old Mr Puddley had hung up and the phone had gone dead. Wilmot just hoped that the old man had understood what was important, that was all.

Publicity.

That's what was needed.

Records weren't records unless they were seen to be set.

12

All in the Jaws

In the lead up to the World Chip Record attempt, the days seemed to alternate between dragging and whizzing by. At one moment the clock hands would take two hours just to move one minute, and then they would move two hours in no time at all.

Wilmot did what he could to get his stomach into shape for the ordeal ahead. He tried to stuff as much into it as possible to stretch it, but was rather restricted in this by his lack of suitable materials. He didn't have the money to go and buy large bags of chips to practise with, and his mum wouldn't give him the extra food he needed for his training.

There were two reasons for this. Firstly, Wilmot's mum didn't know he was in training, because he hadn't told her. And secondly – which was also the reason he hadn't told her – because she wouldn't have approved anyway or have given him more food, even if he'd asked for it.

His mum wouldn't have understood that the World Chip Record was a serious test of endurance and athletic ability. She'd only have seen it as an excuse for Wilmot to stuff himself.

Parents were like that. Not logical.

Being short of the extra food he needed for training his stomach Wilmot did what he could with what was available – eating whatever else he could get his hands on, even when it wasn't strictly speaking food. Grass, for example. He ate a bit of that, but he couldn't have said that he liked it much, and couldn't honestly see why cows were so keen on the stuff.

Then after giving grass a try for a while he gave up on it, and started to eat a few pages from his exercise books instead.

This was as much to strengthen his jaws as anything. For paper needed quite a bit of chewing, and Wilmot knew that if he was to set any sort of half decent World Chip Record, then as much depended on his chewing as it did on his digestion.

Chips had to be chewed, or you couldn't get them down, and strong jaws were essential. Strong jaws and a rapid chewing action, were what he was going to need.

Oh, yes, Wilmot thought, it all looked so simple on the face of it. What could be easier, people thought, than to stuff a few chips into your mouth and wolf them down. But no, once you got into it, it was far more subtle and complicated than that.

Yes, good preparation was essential.

After half a day, Wilmot gave up on eating paper when he accidentally ate his homework. It wasn't until Mr Stevens came to collect it, that Wilmot realised what he had done.

"Where's your homework, Wilmot?" Mr Stevens said.

"I'm afraid I've eaten it," Wilmot said apologetically.

"Eaten it?" Mr Stevens said. "Why? Didn't you get enough for breakfast?"

"I mean I ate it by mistake," Wilmot said.

"Why? What did you mistake it for?"

"I thought it was a blank sheet, but it wasn't."

"And might I ask why you were eating blank sheets of paper in the first place, Wilmot?"

"Em . . . to strengthen up my jaws, Mr Stevens," Wilmot said. "I can explain. You see . . . "

"Do me a favour, Wilmot," Mr Stevens said, "don't! Don't explain. Whenever I hear any of your explanations, Wilmot, I end up more confused than before you started. So don't explain to me,

Wilmot. Don't ever explain anything to me, ever again."

"Yes, Mr Stevens."

"Right. So please re-do your homework and, this time, let me see it before you eat it, okay?"

By the time Friday came, Wilmot reckoned that he was nearing peak condition. He was training now with three packets of bubble gum, which he had managed to get into his mouth all together. The chewing action was building up his jaws a treat.

Then it was Saturday at last. Excitement mounted up in him as the morning passed. Today was the day.

He and Terry followed their usual Saturday morning routine. Breakfast, watch some television, then Wilmot went to his swimming lessons and Terry went to his football. Then round the shops with Mum, then home for lunch, then ...

"What would you like to do this afternoon, you two?" Mum said, as she served up lunch. Wilmot had been in two minds about lunch. Should he eat it or not? Would it fill him up too much, or would it whet his appetite? He decided to eat just a little of it, just to line his stomach.

"I thought I might go round to see Martin, if that's all right," Wilmot said, his story well prepared in advance.

"And I thought I might go round to Dave's," Terry said, giving Wilmot a look.

"Oh ... okay, then," Mum said. "In that case, I'll ring up the hairdresser's and see if I can get my hair done."

But Wilmot didn't go to Martin's, and Terry didn't go to Dave's. And though they didn't know it, Mum didn't go and get her hair done. She felt too tired, and lay down on the sofa instead, with a cup of tea and a packet of biscuits, and she watched an old film on TV, while Dad went to the football to watch his team lose, 1–3.

Wilmot had arranged to meet Martin at Mrs Wilkins's Chip Shop, where he would be waiting with his mum's alarm clock to time the World Chip attempt.

Terry was being quite friendly to Wilmot, which made him nervous. In some ways open hostilities were easier to deal with. You never knew about Terry, whether he was being really friendly, or whether he was just plotting to get you when you least expected it with an Australian Armpit or a Czechoslovakian Crab Claw with Extra Pincers.

As they walked along on their way to the chip shop, Wilmot noticed that Terry had something inside his jacket.

"What's that?" he said.

"Towel," Terry said. "I got it out of the bathroom."

"What for?"

"Because I'm your second, aren't I?" Terry said. "Well, seconds always have towels. Everyone knows that."

"But that's boxing," Wilmot said. "This is chips."

"Chips, boxing, it's all the same," Terry said. "You can't have any sporting event – and especially not world records – without having a bloke with a towel. You look at football, when the trainer runs on because someone's got hurt, he always has a towel and a sponge!" And Terry triumphantly extracted the bath sponge from inside his jacket and held it up for Wilmot to see. "A towel and a sponge, see. You have to have a towel so you can throw it in, if you need to. Throwing in the towel, see. It means you give up. So if you start choking on all the chips, I'll throw in the towel!"

"I'd rather you hit me on the back," Wilmot said.

"No trouble," Terry said. "I'll give you a Burmese Backslap with Double Biffos, or something. That'll see you right. I know all about first aid."

As they approached the chip shop, they saw that Martin was waiting for them outside, his mum's alarm clock in his hand. Mr Puddley, the newspaper reporter from the Herald wasn't there yet, unless he had already gone inside to talk to Mrs Wilkins.

Wilmot was in something of a quandary about the newspaper publicity. He felt that he needed the newspaper coverage to lend authority and recognition to his World Chip Record attempt. But he hadn't actually mentioned anything about it yet to Mum or to Dad. And quite what they might say when they opened up their copy of the Herald the following week to see a photograph of Wilmot stuffing himself with chips, he didn't care to think. But he felt instinctively that they would not approve.

He would just have to hide the paper when it came, that was all. Or better still, tear out the offending page and eat it.

But for now he had to put such trifling worries out of his mind. The time had come for him to compose himself, to be calm, cool, in control and single-minded.

The World Chip Record was only a few bags of chips away. Nothing could stop him now.

13

Count Down

The door was locked, but Mrs Wilkins soon came and opened it up when she heard their knock.

"Come in, Wilmot," she said. "Oh, and Terry and Martin!"

"Martin's the time-keeper and Terry's my second," Wilmot explained. "Terry's brought a towel."

"Oh, fine, fine," Mrs Wilkins said. She had known them all since they were babies and they needed no introduction.

"And I've asked a reporter round from the paper," Wilmot said.

"Oh, have you? Well, he hasn't got here yet, dear. But never mind, come in. I'm just cutting up the last of the potatoes now, and then I'll put on the chips. Come and sit down while they're cooking."

The three boys sat at a table in the old chip shop. An air of sadness seemed to fill it, a sense of things coming to an end. As indeed they were for old Mrs Wilkins, who had spent fifty years with cod and chips and salt and vinegar, and who was now doing so for the last time.

"Lemonade?" Mrs Wilkins said, producing three glasses and a large bottle. "You may as well finish it, or it'll only go to waste."

Terry and Martin drank thirstily, but Wilmot just took a small sip of his. He was saving himself for the chips. He looked down at his T-shirt – Dumbo looked back up at him.

Mrs Wilkins dropped a pan of raw chips into the fat. There was the sizzle, there was the smell. The three boys inhaled deeply. What was there about chips that made you feel so happy, so full of memories? They were as comforting as a hot water bottle on a cold night. Chips. What could beat them?

"Em ... how many are you doing?" Wilmot asked. The last thing he wanted was to run out of chips before the five minutes were up.

"How many do you think you can eat?" Mrs Wilkins said.

Wilmot had given this some thought. There

were on average, sixty chips in one of Mrs Wilkins's large bags of chips, and Wilmot reckoned that he could eat at least two bags a minute. That meant one hundred and twenty chips a minute. Multiply that by five minutes, and it came to six hundred chips exactly. Ten bags.

Wilmot might exceed his own expectations, however, and so would have to keep extra bags in reserve.

"I've done about thirty bags for you," Mrs Wilkins said. "I thought we might as well use all the potatoes up, no sense in them going to waste." Wilmot suddenly began to feel worried. Thirty bags? That was eighteen hundred chips. He'd never eat that, would he?

"Still, what you don't finish, the others can have," Mrs Wilkins said. Terry and Martin seemed quite agreeable to this and poured themselves more lemonade. Mrs Wilkins went to the fridge and brought them another bottle.

The chips were beginning to cook now. Turning from pasty white to light brown. Soon they would be golden brown and ready for eating.

There was a knock at the door and a man entered without waiting to be invited to do so.

"Ah ha!" he said. "So here we are!" He was carrying a very old camera, had a pencil stuck behind his ear and in his other hand he held a reporter's shorthand notebook. "Mrs Wilkins, I presume," he said, as if he had just found her, lost in the jungle.

"Yes?" she said.

"Mr Puddley," he said. "Of the Herald. Come to do a feature on you, and interview you about leaving the community after fifty years of service and dedication to the provision of chips."

"And to see my World Chip Record," Wilmot reminded him. But he didn't seem to hear.

"If I can just ask a few questions and maybe take a photograph or two . . ."

"Right you are. In a minute." Mrs Wilkins said. "Okay then, Wilmot, the chips are nearly ready. I know how many are in there, because I counted them all as I was cutting them. So if we weigh them as well on the scales here, then that way, you'll have the weight, and you'll have the number, and so there can't be any arguing about the record. We just have to take what's left away from what we started with, and then we'll know • how many you've had. Right?"

"Well . . ."

"Right!" Mrs Wilkins said. "Then that's what we'll do."

"Now, I wonder if I could begin by asking you a few simple questions," old Mr Puddley the reporter said. "Now, when did you first start to take an interest in chips?"

"Well," said Wilmot, "I was watching this TV programme ... "

"Not you," old Mr Puddley said sharply. "I was talking to Mrs Wilkins."

"In a minute, dear," Mrs Wilkins said, "I'm busy."

The tension began to fill the room.

"Okay, Wilmot?" Terry said, and he massaged Wilmot's shoulders as Mrs Wilkins weighed and dished up the chips in bags of sixty, and as Martin checked that his clock was working and set to the correct time.

"Yes, okay," Wilmot said. "A bit nervous, but okay."

Terry fanned Wilmot with the towel. He then went over to the sink behind the counter, wet the sponge under the cold tap, and squeezed it out over Wilmot's head.

"Ow!" Wilmot jumped. "It's freezing. What did you do that for?"

"It's what you do when you're a second," Terry said. "Now listen ... "

Mrs Wilkins put a huge plate, piled high with bags of chips, down on the table in front of Wilmot. "I'd let them cool a minute, dear," she said, "or you'll burn your mouth. Now do you want salt and vinegar on them, or ketchup, or both, or what?"

"Just salt and vinegar, please," Wilmot said. He

didn't want to risk ketchup. Not in a world record. Things could get too messy.

Mrs Wilkins put salt and vinegar on the chips. Terry continued with what he was saying.

" . . . now, listen, Wilmot," he said, "I want you to go in there, and I want you to attack. I want you to take the lead with these chips, and I want to see you fight it your way. I want to see you chewing and chomping all the time, and I want to see that left hand working, picking up those chips. Okay?"

"Okay," said Wilmot. "Right. Gotcha."

"I don't want to see you backing off at any time, Wilmot, you got me? You're a good strong boy, with a useful pair of jaws, and you've trained hard for this contest. And I don't want to see you throw it away at the last moment due to an attack of nerves. Right?"

"Right, Ter," said Wilmot.

"Okay. Now remember to keep your guard up and defend yourself at all times. Good luck, Wilmot, and let's go!" And so saying, Terry fanned Wilmot a few more times with the towel and squeezed another sponge full of cold water over his head.

The chips cooled and the tension mounted.

"More lemonade, Wilmot?" Mrs Wilkins asked. "Is he allowed to have a drink with it, or not?"

"Just water, please," he said. "Nothing fizzy."

"No, nothing fizzy," Terry agreed. "We don't want him to explode. Not with thirty bags of chips inside him. We'd never get it all off the walls."

Mrs Wilkins poured out a tumbler of water and brought it over to the table. Mr Puddley from the Herald, was still trying to interview her, but with limited success.

"And so do you remember the day when you cooked your first bit of fish, Mrs Wilkins?"

"Shhh!" she told him. "Afterwards."

Silence fell in the chip shop. The only sound was the sizzling of the fat as it cooled down in the fryer. No more would Mrs Wilkins peel the potatoes for her traditional handmade chips. No more would she make up the batter for the cod, and dip each piece of fish into it, holding it by the tail, and then flicking it – with a skill born of experience – over her shoulder and into the fryer. It was time to move on.

"Ten!" Martin was counting down. He sat gripping his mum's alarm clock, and watching the second hand intently.

"Nine!"

Wilmot flexed his fingers and cracked his knuckles. The sound echoed round the chip shop like gunfire.

"Eight!"

Terry fanned Wilmot with the towel. Then he fanned himself. Then he fanned Mrs Wilkins, then Martin, then Mr Puddley from the Herald.

"Don't!" Mr Puddley said. "It makes a draught!"

"Seven!"

Suddenly Wilmot wished that he had gone to the toilet. But never mind, he'd just have to last out. It was too late now.

"Six!"

No turning back now.

"Five!"

Something happened. Something was happening. Something terrible was happening. Wilmot couldn't swallow. His swallow wasn't working. His mouth was dry as a desert in summer and his swallow wouldn't work any more!

"Four!"

He reached for the glass of water and drank. It was okay. His swallow had come back.

"Three!"

Two to go then.

"Two!"

And Mrs Wilkins cried, "Good luck, Wilmot!"

"One!"

Well, this was it then.

"Lift off!"

And he was away.

14

The World Chip Record

It was a sight to see and no doubt about it. It was one of the wonders of the modern world, was Wilmot at his chips. It wasn't a pretty sight, not by any means. In fact, all things considered, it was rather disgusting. But it was definitely a sight worth seeing at least once before you died.

Wilmot had decided not to bother with a fork, and had elected to use his fingers. When it came to the off, it was more hands than fingers though, and he grabbed up handfuls of chips with both hands.

His right hand stuffed in one load of chips while his left hand picked up another. His left hand put a load in then, while the right gathered up replenishments. And all the while his jaws chomp-chomp-chomped. They went neither fast, nor slow, but with a steady mechanical rhythm, rather like a mechanical digger, eating a trench into a road.

Manners didn't come into it. And if Mum had been there to see Wilmot at his World Chip Record attempt, she would probably have died of shame. Chips and bits of chips flew everywhere. Half chewed chips were on display as Wilmot opened his mouth wide to cram in more. There was none of this 'Don't eat with your mouth open'. There was no 'Chew your food properly before you swallow it, Wilmot'. It was all sheer primitive savagery.

Cavemen probably ate like that, Martin thought, as he watched Wilmot grab another two handfuls of chips, and shovel them in. And they probably all looked like Wilmot, only hairier.

I never knew he had it in him, Terry thought. Never! Who would ever have dreamed that his own brother was capable of such acts. For Wilmot was scoffing chips like a hero.

"One!" Martin said, keeping an eye on the clock.

Martin shouting like that momentarily put Wilmot off his stride and he lost the rhythm of the chips. He faltered. His confidence ebbed. What did Martin mean? Did he mean one minute had gone? Or did he mean that Wilmot had only eaten one bag of chips?

Martin seemed to understand Wilmot's confusion and cleared up the matter immediately. "One minute gone," he said. "Four bags down. Twenty six to go."

Four bags, that wasn't bad. Four bags in one minute, it was incredible. One bag every fifteen seconds. Sixty chips to the bag. That was four chips every second. It was good going all right, but he wanted to do better. There was only one solution – bigger handfuls, stuff them in quicker, and less chewing.

Wilmot took a quick swig of water and pressed on.

Mrs Wilkins topped up his glass from a water jug and watched in admiration as two more handfuls of chips made their way towards Wilmot's cake hole. Not that it was a cake hole now. It was a chip hole. A sort of black hole, like out in space, into which chips fell, never to be seen again.

It was a good send-off, she thought. A fitting memorial to her fifty years behind the counter and to a lifetime in the business. The council would probably put a brass plate up outside on the wall, when she had gone. It would read something like:

Formerly Wilkins's Chip Shop.
It was on these premises that the World Chip Record was established by Wilmot Tanner, whilst eating Mrs Wilkins's famous chips.

Yes, it was a nice feeling, Mrs Wilkins thought, to leave a little something behind you. She had given her whole life to chips, and now that here she was in her twilight years, about to retire to the Isle of Wight, chips were giving her something back.

On went Wilmot, steadily, surely, mechanically as ever. He thought that swimming across the Channel must be like this. One stroke after another, one chew after another. One stroke after another, one swallow after another. Grab, chew, swallow. Grab, chew, swallow. Steady plodding, that was what accomplished things. It wasn't anything flashy, the secret was steady work. He could have been a robot, from the way he moved, were it not for the beads of sweat starting to appear on his forehead, which proved that far from being iron and steel and microchips, he was flesh and blood.

Terry saw the sweat appear and held his towel at the ready. He fanned Wilmot to cool him down, and Wilmot nodded gratefully.

"Two!" Martin shouted. "Two minutes gone! Nine bags down! Twenty one to go!"

Nine bags, that was good. Wilmot was getting faster. He had feared that he would slow up the more he ate. But the opposite was proving the case. He had eaten nine bags of chips already, and believe it or not, he actually felt hungry. More, he thought, more chips!

Terry interpreted the hungry look of grim determination in Wilmot's eyes to mean that he wanted another sponge full of cold water squeezed over his head and he readily obliged.

"Grrr!" Wilmot said, as Terry soaked him. It was the last thing he wanted. He'd have told Terry to get lost, only he couldn't spare the precious seconds from chewing. So, "Grrrr!" he said again, hoping that Terry would get the message. But he didn't.

"You're welcome, Wilmot," he said. "I'll get you another one."

"Grrrr!" said Wilmot. But it was no use. Terry went and ran the sponge under the cold tap once more, and came and dunked him again.

"Three minutes!" Martin shouted. "And fifteen bags! Fifteen bags down, fifteen to go!"

That was good. That was very good. Even faster than the last time. He was getting the chips down him like nobody's business. If only Wilmot could keep it up, if only he could ... only he didn't know if he'd be able to. He was starting to feel, well ... a bit ill.

Mr Puddley, the reporter from the Herald, was not quite sure what to do. He had really come to interview Mrs Wilkins about her fifty years behind the chip counter, and to take a couple of pictures. People liked to read about that sort of story, he knew as much from experience. The Herald was a local paper, and stories like this were of local colour.

But now that he was here, Mr Puddley had to admit that the World Chip attempt was a good story. The reporter in him took over. This wasn't just local colour, this World Chip Record, it was more than that. It was news.

He got his old camera out of its case and fitted a flash bulb into it, ready to take a photograph. He ought to buy a new camera, really, for he had only six flash bulbs left. Once they were gone, he wouldn't be able to use the camera any more, for nobody seemed to sell flash bulbs now and hadn't done for years.

He lifted the camera and focused it on Wilmot as he raised another handful of chips to his mouth. He wasn't sure though. The shot didn't quite seem dramatic enough. It needed another element somehow. Still, never mind, he'd take it anyway.

Flash!

For a moment Wilmot was blinded and couldn't see the chip plate in front of him. It didn't matter though, he was running on autopilot now anyway. He could eat them with his eyes shut.

He did feel a bit ill though, that was the only thing. His stomach, which had felt so empty, now suddenly felt enormously full. It struck him for the first time that what he was doing might actually be a bit, well, dangerous – stupid, even. Yes, stupid. That was how it suddenly seemed. Like not such a good idea after all.

"Four minutes and twenty one bags!" Martin said. "Sixty seconds and nine bags to go!"

Wilmot reached out for more chips. Sixty seconds was a long tunnel that he had to go down, and the light at the end of it was far, far away.

"Another sponge, Wilmot?" Terry offered. But Wilmot managed to shake his head. Wilmot was slowing now, slowing, like an engine that has run out of steam. Just keep going, that was all he could do. It was best not to think of anything. Not of chips or world records or the time left or anything. Just keep moving his jaws, up and down, and keep on doing it in the belief that an hour from now, or a day from now, or a year from now, Martin would look at the clock and shout, "Time's up!"

That was it. Done. Wilmot swallowed the last of the chips in his mouth and slumped back in his chair. His stomach felt like a bag of cement. Everyone moved forward to congratulate him.

"Well done, Wilmot," Terry said, "I knew you'd

do it! Well done, Wilmot ... " But something was wrong! Terry saw it at once. Wilmot's eyes had turned glassy and his face was going red. He was spluttering and coughing and he looked like he might pop.

He was choking. On a chip.

"It's all right, Wilmot, don't panic!" Terry said. "Don't worry, bros! It's all right. I know just what to do!"

The others had also noticed that something was wrong.

"Do something!" Mrs Wilkins shouted. "He's choking, somebody do something! Oh, where's my book on first aid." She turned to Mr Puddley. "You're a reporter," she said. "You must have been in these kinds of emergency situations before. Do something."

"Right you are," Mr Puddley said obligingly. "I'll take his photograph." He quickly fitted a fresh flash bulb into his camera, pointed it at the choking and spluttering Wilmot and said, "Watch the birdie now, smile please!"

"That's no good!" Mrs Wilkins said. "Get your fingers down his throat!"

"It's all right," Terry said. "I know what to do!"

So saying, Terry pulled Wilmot up to his feet, stood behind him, wrapped his arms around Wilmot's chest and gave him the most sudden and forceful bear hug. For a moment Wilmot's eyeballs looked even more likely to pop. Terry squeezed again. This time Wilmot stopped spluttering, and a small chip popped out of his mouth, and as it did, a flash bulb popped and the two brothers were dazzled.

"Lovely," Mr Puddley said. "Lovely shot. I might even have got the chip in it."

Terry dumped Wilmot down on to his seat, and then sat to get his breath himself.

"Thanks, Terry," Wilmot said. "I think you saved my life."

"That's all right, Wilmot," Terry said. "It was just a little thing I've been working on. I knew it would come in useful one day."

"Why? What was it exactly, dear?" Mrs Wilkins asked. "Was it something you learned in first aid?"

"No," Terry said modestly. "It was a Swaziland Squash with Extra Strangles, actually. I've been practising it on the cat."

"I hope the cat's all right then," Mrs Wilkins said. "Because it did look most ferocious."

"He's fine," Terry said. "I got a fishbone out of his throat. And two thorns out of his paws as well."

Wilmot had recovered enough to speak. He took a sip of water first, and then said "Well? How did I do?"

"Twenty five," Martin said. "Twenty five bags in five minutes! Genius, Wilmot, sheer genius!"

"Less the one chip he choked on," Terry said. "You can't count that, as he didn't swallow it. It went flying across the room."

"No, I've allowed for that," Martin said. "That's twenty five bags not counting that one. So that means an average of five bags a minute, or one bag every twelve seconds, or five chips a second. Well done, Wilmot! It's a record."

Wilmot smiled faintly.

He hoped it was a record.

It certainly felt like it.

15

The World Stomach Ache Record

They walked home very slowly.

"I'm going to spend the rest of my life on the toilet," Wilmot said.

"Never mind," said Terry, "I'll come and visit you every now and again. And you have got the world record. You must have."

Martin turned off when they reached the top of his street. He wanted to get his mum's alarm clock back before she missed it.

"Thanks, Martin," Wilmot said, "for doing the time-keeping and everything."

"Pleasure," Martin said. "I enjoyed it. Tell me when you're going to try for any more records, and I'll come and time them, too. Cheers then, Wilmot. Bye, Terry. See you Monday." And he walked off towards his house.

Terry and Wilmot went slowly on their way.

"Look at your stomach," Terry said. "You look like you're having a baby . . . well, twins really."

Wilmot looked down. His T-shirt looked strained and the picture of Dumbo bulged out alarmingly.

"That was a good choice," Terry said. "Wearing your Dumbo T-shirt. Because you look about as fat as an elephant. All you need's the trunk, really, and you could get a job at the circus."

"If you don't belt up," Wilmot said, "I'm going to give you a Tunisian Finger in the Ear-Hole." But it was obvious to both him and to Terry that he was capable of no such thing.

At last they got to their garden gate.

"Not a word to Mum," Wilmot said, "about the world record."

"But she'll see it in the paper when it comes out, won't she?" Terry said.

"Yes, well, maybe so. But don't say anything yet. I'll have to prepare the ground. So we'll just carry on as normal, eh, Terry? Nothing suspicious."

"You don't look very normal," Terry said. For not only was Wilmot's tummy straining at his T-shirt as though he was having a baby, he had also gone rather green in the face, and he smelt very strongly of vinegar.

"I don't feel it," Wilmot said. "I just hope I feel better soon. And not a word, mind."

"Not a word," Terry said. "Rely on me." And he hid the towel inside his jacket, so that Mum wouldn't see it, and wonder what he had been using it for.

"Thanks for helping though," Wilmot said. "And being my second."

"S'all right," Terry said, a little embarrassed.

Sometimes it was easier to fight. Funnily enough, being friends with each other made them both feel a bit strange. It was nice, but it was well . . . an odd feeling. Things would be easier when normal hostilities resumed.

They went into the kitchen. Mum was there.

"Ah, good," she said. "You're back together. Dad's just back from the football, too, and I'm doing the tea."

"Great," said Terry. "I'm starving. What is it?"

"It's your favourite," Mum said, "chips!"

"Excuse me," said Wilmot, "I think I need to go to the bathroom."

He didn't eat any tea that night, nor any breakfast the next morning. Mum said she thought he didn't look well, and gave him some fizzy salts to drink, but he poured it down the toilet.

When Wilmot couldn't manage any Sunday lunch either, Mum began to get really worried and said that if things didn't improve by tomorrow, she was going to take him to the doctor. Dad said it was probably no more than a tummy bug and that it probably wasn't anything serious and was most likely due to something Wilmot had eaten.

He was right there.

But Wilmot didn't say anything.

When Sunday tea time came, Wilmot tried to manage a little something for appearances' sake, but he couldn't really get anything down, and just sort of rearranged the food on his plate to make it look as though he had eaten something.

Mum wasn't fooled by this though, and asked to see his stomach. Wilmot lifted his T-shirt and she and Dad stared at it.

"It does look swollen," Mum said.

Dad prodded Wilmot's swollen stomach with his finger.

"Yes ... " he mused, " ... it looks like you've got a sack of chips in there, Wilmot."

But Wilmot still didn't say anything.

By Monday morning, he was starting to feel a little better and he managed a bowl of cornflakes. He said no to the toast, but he knew that he had to eat something or Mum would take him to the doctor. He didn't know whether doctors could tell by looking at your stomach that you had eaten twenty five bags of chips at one sitting, but he wouldn't put it past them.

"Okay, well as you've managed your corn flakes, and if you say that you feel all right ... "

"I do, honestly, I'm fine."

"Well, okay then, you can go to school. But make sure you eat your lunch."

Wilmot didn't eat his lunch, though. He gave it away to a man who was sitting on the pavement outside the newsagent's with a 'Hungry and Homeless' sign on the ground in front of him.

"Are you really hungry?" Wilmot asked.

"Starving," the man said.

"Would you like my lunch?" Wilmot offered.

"Well, if you're sure you don't want it."

"No, not really. I had twenty five bags of chips on Saturday, and I'm still getting over it." He gave the man his sandwich and apple and biscuit from his lunch box.

"Twenty five bags of chips?" the Hungry and Homeless man said. "That sounds like a record."

"It is!" Wilmot said. "I hope."

When Wilmot got to school it was to discover that Martin Fields had told practically everyone all about his attempt on the World Record, and how he had managed twenty five bags of chips at one sitting. But as he hadn't asked Martin not to tell anyone, he could hardly blame him.

Small boys from the infant classes came up to
him in the playground. The braver ones asked for
his autograph, the more timid ones just stood
and looked at him, their jaws hanging open, and
saying, "Twenty five bags of chips. Twenty five
bags of chips," over and over again.

The way rumours went round the school, it was
only a matter of time before the teachers got to
hear of it and Mr Stevens came up to Wilmot
during break and collared him.

"Wilmot," he said, "why's your stomach so big
today?"

"Dunno," Wilmot said. He looked down at his
stomach. It was smaller than it had been on Saturday, but it was still quite large.

"I've been hearing tales of certain adventures
concerning you and twenty five bags of chips,
Wilmot. Anything in this?"

Wilmot looked shifty. But then he always did
when Mr Stevens spoke to him.

"It's . . . it's news to me, Mr Stevens," he said.

"Hmm . . ." Mr Stevens said. "Well, true or false,
Wilmot, all I have to say is *don't ever do it again*!
Gluttony is not to be encouraged. Do you know
what gluttony is, Wilmot?"

"Not exactly, Mr Stevens."

"Twenty five bags of chips at one sitting,

Wilmot, that's gluttony. In fact it's more than that – it's sheer idiocy!"

"Yes, Mr Stevens," Wilmot said.

"You could have killed yourself!"

"Yes, Mr Stevens."

"Right."

Martin came up to Wilmot during the lunch break. "Not eating, then?" he said.

"No," Wilmot said.

"Is it going down?" Martin asked, looking at Wilmot's stomach.

"Gradually."

"So when do you get your name in the record books?" Martin said.

"I'm going to write to them tonight," Wilmot said. "But I'll need you to sign a witness statement."

"A what?" Martin asked.

"Here," Wilmot said. And he showed Martin a paper he had prepared.

The Witness Statement read as follows:

We, the undersigned, do solemnly swear that we were witnesses on Saturday, 24th September at Mrs Wilkins's Chip Shop, when Wilmot Tanner set the World Record for Chips, by eating twenty five bags of chips, each containing sixty chips, making a total of . . . and there were a lot of

calculations and crossings out here ... *a total
of one thousand five hundred chips in five
minutes flat exactly.*
Signed – Second:
    Time-keeper:
    Mrs Wilkins:

Martin signed his name next to Time-keeper,
and then Wilmot went and found Terry and got
him to sign his name next to Second. On his way
home from school, he called in on Mrs Wilkins, to
find her surrounded by boxes and bags and pack-
ing cases, as she prepared for her move to the Isle
of Wight. There was a notice on the window of the
chip shop saying *Closed for Good*.

Mrs Wilkins signed the Witness Statement, and
she and Wilmot said goodbye.

He went home then to write a covering letter
to go with the Witness Statement, and he
addressed the letter to the editor of the *World
Book of Records* – who was yet to reply to Wilmot's
first letter, about his having the world record for
running round the back garden. He put the letter
into his school folder, intending to post it the next
morning.

And that, by rights, should have been it, and
here is where the story should have ended. Wilmot
should have got his name into the record books

for holding the World Record for Chips, and as a result, he should have become rich and famous, and have lived happily ever after.

But here's what really happened instead.

16

Chips not Included

When Wilmot woke on Tuesday morning, the first thing he did was to inspect his stomach, to see whether it was on its way back to normal. Fortunately it was. The worst of the chips had worn off, and within a few days he ought to be back to being skinny.

He dressed then, and went down for breakfast, after first checking that the letter he had to post was in his folder. As he got to the kitchen, Mum came through from the hall, carrying the mail.

"Postman's been," she said, "and there's one for you, Wilmot."

"For me?" Wilmot said. "Me?" He never usually got letters, except at Christmas and on his birthday.

"That's not fair," Terry said. "Where's mine? It's

not fair that he should get a letter and I shouldn't."

"It's hardly my fault," Mum said. "I didn't send it to him, did I?"

"It's not fair all the same," Terry said. "I deserve a letter more than he does. I'm better looking." He turned to Wilmot. "Want me to open it for you?" he said, reaching out for the letter.

"No!" Wilmot said, and snatched his letter back.

"So what's it say then?" Terry demanded.

"Mind your own," Wilmot told him.

"Aren't you going to open it then?"

"Not while you're here."

"I'll get you," Terry said.

"I'll get you back," Wilmot told him.

"I'll get you back for getting me back," Terry said.

"Then I'll get you back for getting me back for getting you back!"

"Then I'll get you back for . . ."

"Please!" said Mum. "Be quiet, or . . ."

"Or what?" Terry said.

"I'll get you," Mum said.

After breakfast – he managed the cornflakes and half the toast this time – Wilmot hurried to his room to read the letter before going to school.

He studied the envelope first. It was a proper letter, with Wilmot's name and address typed on it, neatly and with no spelling mistakes. It almost looked official. Wilmot tore it open with care, slid out the paper inside and unfolded it.

The letter inside was typed on headed notepaper. The heading was very stylish and grand, and it read World Record Book Publishing Ltd, 38 Foxglove Lane, London. Wilmot's heart pounded with excitement. They had finally written back to him about his sixty laps round the garden. What with that and the chips, maybe his name would go into the record books *twice*!

His fingers unsteady, Wilmot held the letter out to read it, saw it was the wrong way up, righted it, and read.

Dear Mr Tanner,

Thank you for your letter of the 3rd, informing us of your success in running round the back garden sixty times in twenty seven minutes and suggesting that we include this feat in our next edition of The World Record Book.

Unfortunately, we receive many letters such as yours, and it is with regret that I shall have to decline your offer to include you. The records we publish are all based on some kind of measurable standard, and I fear that as no

two back gardens are ever the same, such a
standard would not exist in this case.

Wilmot put the letter down, then picked it up
again with a sinking heart. He heard Mum shouting up from downstairs, calling him to come and
put his shoes on as it was time to go to school.
But he had to finish the letter, and read on.

I must stress that ours is not the book in which
to find details of weird one-off stunts, and it
is always best to check with us in advance,
before undertaking a new record attempt. It
is not our policy to include any records which
could be considered as harmful, unhealthy or
potentially dangerous. Such activities as, for
example, sword swallowing, going over Nia-
gara Falls in a barrel, or attempting to con-
sume large quantities of either food or drink
in a limited period of time. Records for eating
jellied eels, oysters, chocolate bars or chips, for
example, would not be included.
  Good luck with your future endeavours.
                              Yours sincerely,
                          P. Matthias Editor

Wilmot almost dropped the letter. He read the
word again. *Chips*! They wouldn't include it! They

wouldn't include his chips. Not one chip. Not one solitary chip. Not so much as one single chip among the whole twenty five bags. All that training, that preparation, that organisation, all that eating, all that stomach ache and all that time sitting in the bathroom afterwards, and all for what? For nothing.

Chips would not be included!

"Wilmot! Come on, or you'll be late!"

He didn't care. He didn't care if he was late forever. He didn't care if he lived the rest of his life five minutes behind everyone else. What did it all matter now? Success had crumbled to failure right in front of his eyes. He would never get into the record books now, not for anything. There was nothing he was good at – or rather what he was good at was not appreciated. He couldn't sing, he couldn't dance, he couldn't tell funny stories. He couldn't play a musical instrument, he wasn't that good at football and he wasn't all that great at school. But there were two things in his life that Wilmot had shown real promise at – at running round the garden and at eating chips. But did he get the recognition he deserved for it? No, he did not. The world was against him. Everything he did was wrong. Some people won prizes for just smiling, but not Wilmot. Nothing that he

ever did was right. The simple truth was, he had
had his chips.

"WILMOT!"

"Coming!" he said. He took the letter he had
been going to post out from his school folder,
ripped it up and hid the pieces in a drawer. No
sense in sending that now. He closed the door of
his bedroom and dragged himself somehow down
the stairs.

"Wilmot, you're going to be late!"

"Yes, Mum," he said. And so what if he was?

"Are you all right?"

"Fine."

He put his shoes on as though he were pulling
on lead boots which were to drag him to the
bottom of the river.

"Be quick then, Terry's waiting for you at the
gate."

Mum kissed him, but he didn't feel it. He
walked outside. There must have been sunlight
there, but he didn't see it. There must have been
ground under his feet, but he could never recollect
walking on any of it.

"What's up?" Terry said. But Wilmot didn't
answer. He looked at his hand and saw that the
letter was still in it, and he gave his brother
the letter to read. Terry read it quickly and then
looked across at Wilmot as they walked along.

"What rotten luck, Wilmot," he said. "What terrible rotten luck. All those chips for nothing."

"I'll never be famous now," Wilmot said. "Never."

He looked so miserable and crest-fallen that Terry put his arm around Wilmot's shoulders. And Wilmot almost cried. But he didn't.

They walked on to school, silent for most of the way.

"But you can't give up, Wilmot, you can't give up now."

"Yes, I can," Wilmot said. "I'm giving up forever." But even as he was saying it, Wilmot knew that he didn't really mean it. The embers of his old determination were still glowing inside him. It would take more than a few knock-backs to finish Wilmot off. He'd do it yet. He'd show them. He'd see his name up there in print if it took him till he was sixty. Or seventy or eighty. Or a hundred and ten.

Yes, maybe that was it. Maybe he should try and get the record for the world's oldest man.

17

Terry the Hero

It was Friday when the Herald, the local free newspaper, fell through the letter box. Wilmot had forgotten all about the reporter being at Mrs Wilkins's during the World Chip Record attempt, and the photographs he had taken – what with all his other woes occupying his mind – and he hurried to pick the paper up before anyone else in the house got to it.

Wilmot's World Chip Record was still a record, as far as he was concerned, even if the record book wouldn't recognise it. And there was a chance now of local – if not international – fame if the pictures had been printed and the story told. Perhaps when they saw the story, the television people might come round.

But even here, Wilmot was cheated of his glory. There was no mention of his World Chip Record at all. All he could find was a long boring story all about Mrs Wilkins retiring to the Isle of Wight, and how she had spent fifty years serving the community with her potato peeler. Underneath the story was a picture of Mrs Wilkins with a potato in one hand and a bottle of sauce in the other, and the caption read: *'I'll have time to ketchup on my reading now,' says Mrs Wilkins, who retires today after fifty years behind the counter.*

Wilmot turned the page in disgust. It was shameful the way he was ignored.

But wait a minute! There he was. *There he was*! Right there was a picture of Wilmot in Mrs Wilkins's Chip Shop. Wilmot and Terry together. Terry had Wilmot in a sort of bear hug, and, flying through the air as if it had just come from Wilmot's mouth, was a chip.

This time the caption under the picture read *Brothers In Chip Drama. For full story, see below.*

Wilmot looked down for the full story.

Quick thinking and fast acting Terry Tanner saved his brother Wilmot from certain death today when a chip got stuck in Wilmot's throat. Clever Terry, who is a first aid expert, administered a Swaziland Squash with Extra Strangles to dislodge the chip which was causing Wilmot to choke. Terry said that he had

*practised on the cat, and had saved its life
too. Grateful Wilmot said, 'I think my brother
is smashing. He is the tops.'*

What? thought Wilmot. He had said no such
thing. The reporter had made that up. It was
probably all Terry's fault that he had choked
anyway, soaking him with sponges and waving
towels at him.

*The incident happened at Mrs Wilkins's Chip
Shop on the afternoon of her retirement party,
when the boys had called round to say cheerio,
and to wish her a happy retirement.*

Wilmot could not believe it. He *could not* believe
it! There wasn't a word of truth in the whole
thing. And no mention of his World Chip Record
anywhere. Well, if that was the newspapers, you
could keep them. He'd never believe a word he
read in any of them again. He was going to bin
this one, right now, before ...

"What's that, Wilmot?"

Too late. He looked round. Mum was at his
shoulder, staring wide-eyed at the photograph of
him and Terry in the paper.

"Wilmot!" she said. "So that's why you were
feeling ill when you came home on Saturday!" She

reached out and took the paper from him. "And you never said. Either of you! And Terry saved your life! Honestly! You pair! I just don't know about you two sometimes."

"Em ... we didn't want to worry you," Wilmot mumbled.

"Oh, Wilmot, honestly! And Terry too, not saying anything. Keeping it all to himself. So modest and everything, and not telling a soul. Oh, your brother really is a hero, Wilmot, don't you think?"

"Yes, Mum," Wilmot muttered. For how could he say otherwise?

They came round with the television cameras then. But it wasn't to see Wilmot. Not really. They wanted a very quick word with him, asking him to say how grateful to Terry he was for Terry saving his life. And then they wanted him to stand there, pretending to die, so that Terry could demonstrate the Swaziland Squash with Extra Strangles on him for the benefit of the cameras. But it wasn't really Wilmot they wanted to see at all. It was Terry. And then they wanted Terry to do the same to the cat, so he could show how he had saved the cat's life as well. Only the cat went and ran up a drainpipe and Wilmot wished he could do the same.

And once Terry had been on the television, he started to get letters from everyone, telling him what a brave boy he was. And there was even talk for a while of him being offered his own chat show on Children's TV, though it came to nothing in the end – thank goodness.

It went to Terry's head, of course – it would have gone to anyone's – and he became quite insufferable, and began to think that he really was special. Even Mum and Dad – who were very proud of him – began to notice the change in him, and Dad said that if Terry's head got any bigger, they would have to move to another house to fit it in.

Terry got so big-headed for a while that Wilmot had to get him in a corner once or twice, when no one was looking, and give him a Hungarian Head Butt, plus a Tasmanian Hard Boiled Egg with Extra Spoons, just to bring him back to his senses.

Of course, nothing lasts forever and, after a week or two, people forgot about Terry and became interested in something else. Not that Terry forgot about Terry. He still saw himself as the centre of attention, and it took him almost two months to get back to normal. Not that even a normal Terry was up to that much.

Wilmot wasn't idle during that two months. He worked quietly and persistently away in the background. If he wasn't to be allowed to set new records, he would try to break old ones. He took out his World Book of Records to see what he could do. He tried to break the world record for spitting water melon seeds – but his spitting wasn't strong enough. He tried to break the world record for standing in one place – 17 years – but Mum told him that he couldn't just stand there for 17 years, as she needed to vacuum the spot he was standing on.

He tried to break the world record for making a paper chain – 36 miles long – but he ran out of paper. He tried to break the world record for blowing a bubble with bubble gum – 55 cms wide. But his bubble burst when it got to 25 cms, and exploded all over him. He ended up with bubble gum stuck in his hair and up his nose, and Mum had to put him in the bath and give him a shampoo. He tried to beat the world plate spinning record, but he dropped the plates. He tried to beat the world egg juggling record, but yes, he dropped the eggs – and he hadn't used hard boiled ones either.

But he didn't give up. He didn't succeed, but he didn't give up. He would never give up, not Wilmot.

18

Wilmot at Last

At length Wilmot's attempts to break a world record – any world record – became so wearing that his mum had to write to the World Book of Records to see if they could help, or suggest anything to cure Wilmot of his compulsion.

They wrote back, within a few days this time, and it wasn't the usual envelope that arrived, but a large brown one, with a cardboard back, so that whatever was inside wouldn't get bent or damaged.

"What's that?" Wilmot said.

"Wait and see," Mum said. She opened the envelope and read the letter. Then she reached inside and took out something else. It was a beautiful parchment document, headed in gold lettering, and with a wax seal on it, and lots of beautiful writing.

"Here, Wilmot," Mum said. "That's for you."

"Me?" Wilmot said. "What is it?"

"Read it and see."

He did. The gold lettering on the document read *World Book of Records Certificate* and under that Wilmot saw his own name, written in copperplate handwriting, as though with an old quill pen. He read on, and what he saw said:

This is to certify that Wilmot Tanner has been given a unique and special AWARD *for his attempts to break world records and to enter the World Book of Records. No one has applied himself with more enthusiasm, persistence, skill and dedication than Wilmot, and in the face of much adversity and disappointment, Wilmot has never given up.*

It is with pride and pleasure, therefore, that we present Wilmot with this certificate as proof and evidence of the fact that Wilmot currently holds the World Record for Trying.

Congratulations.

Signed,

P. Mathias. Ed. The World Book of Records.

148

Mum looked at Wilmot. He was a curious sight. His chest seemed to puff out, even as she watched him, the way a robin puffs its feathers out in the cold.

"Pleased?" she said.

"I've got one!" Wilmot said. "I knew I would. I've got one – a world record. I'm going to frame this and hang it up in my room."

"Are you happy then? No more bubble gum? No more broken eggs? No more broken plates? No more standing in a corner for 17 years?"

"Yes," said Wilmot. "Happy – for now."

Terry wasn't that impressed, but then Wilmot didn't really expect him to be. In fact Wilmot reckoned Terry was a bit jealous, because he tried to give him a Rumanian Rat Bite with Double Molars when he wasn't looking. But Wilmot fended him off with a Scottish Dentist Hold, and made a run for it before Terry could try anything else.

Wilmot just happened to be walking round the back garden with his certificate – he wasn't *really* looking for people to show it to – when Mr Ronson peered over the fence and Wilmot asked him if he would like to see his World Record for Trying certificate. And Mr Ronson said that he would. He held it up and admired it greatly, and said that Wilmot was a very clever boy. And when Mr

Ronson said that, Wilmot started to think that maybe Mr Ronson wasn't such a boring old liar after all.

But he was wrong.

For instead of giving Wilmot his certificate back so that he could get off into the house, Mr Ronson seemed to forget that he had hold of it and began on one of his stories. And it was clear that Wilmot wasn't going to get his certificate back until Mr Ronson had finished.

"Yes, it puts me in mind of when I was back in the army," he said.

"What does?" Wilmot said.

"Your certificate here," Mr Ronson said.

"Oh, yes," Wilmot said. "Well, don't feel you have to . . ."

"Oh, no trouble," Mr Ronson said. "You're not in a hurry, are you?"

"Yes," Wilmot said.

"Good," Mr Ronson said, and he got his pipe out of his cardigan pocket and put his elbow on the fence. "It was back in the war," he said.

"Which one?"

"One of them," Mr Ronson said. "I've been in so many in my time. Anyway, I had this mate called Peeler Hargreaves, who was a private in the Catering Corp . . ."

Wilmot actually fell asleep then, fast asleep

against the garden fence. When he woke up, it was starting to get dark and Mr Ronson was still talking.

". . . and that's the reason why from that day till this, he's always walked with a limp. And that, Wilmot, is a true story." Mr Ronson didn't seem to notice that Wilmot had been asleep at all. "As true as I'm standing here," Mr Ronson said. "Oh, here's your certificate back, Wilmot. Well done. Well, if you'll excuse me then, I must go and put some fertiliser on my sprouts."

Mr Ronson went off to tend to his vegetables. Wilmot took his certificate and turned to go indoors. He stopped and looked back at Mr Ronson, who was bent over his compost. Wilmot wondered if Mr Ronson had ever tried to get into the record books himself. He felt sure that there would be a vacancy for him in there. He probably held the World Record for Boring People to Death.

Wilmot went into the house then, and up to his room. He framed his World Record for Trying Certificate and hung it up on a nail.

No one could ever take that away from him.

Never.

It would be his until the day he died, and maybe even long after he had gone.

He had tried. And that's what counted. More than anything. In the end.